D1195565

The Wolf's Tooth

Also by G. Clifton Wisler

The Wolf's Tooth

G. Clifton Wisler

Lodestar Books   E. P. Dutton   New York

Copyright © 1987 by G. Clifton Wisler

Library of Congress Cataloging in Publication Data

Wisler, G. Clifton.
  The wolf's tooth.

  "Lodestar books."
  Summary: When Elias moves to an Indian reservation
on the Texas frontier, where his father will be a
schoolteacher, he shares many adventures with a
Tonkawa Indian boy.
  [1. Friendship—Fiction. 2. Frontier and pioneer
life—Fiction. 3. Tonkawa Indians—Fiction. 4. Indians
of North America—Fiction. 5. Texas—Fiction] I. Title.
PZ7.W78033Wo 1987 [Fic] 87-543
ISBN 0-525-67197-8

Published in the United States by E. P. Dutton,
2 Park Avenue, New York, N.Y. 10016,
a subsidiary of NAL Penguin Inc.

Published simultaneously in Canada by
Fitzhenry & Whiteside Limited, Toronto

Editor: Rosemary Brosnan

Printed in the U.S.A.   W   First Edition
10 9 8 7 6 5 4 3 2 1

for Margaret

1.

The bed of the supply wagon lurched and groaned as the wheels first sank into the sandy soil, then drove themselves against the sandstone rocks of the makeshift road. The road was really no more than a trace torn by wheel ruts through the gulches and hillsides of the Brazos country. Now that summer had arrived, the buffalo grass had close to erased it in places. Here and there a juniper sapling fought to obstruct it entirely, only to crack beneath the hooves of the army mules.

In the center of the wagon bed, bouncing along with sacks of flour and kegs of nails, Elias gazed in dismay at the bleak countryside. Since leaving the cluster of stone buildings that made up the army post at Fort Belknap, he'd seen nothing but broad grassland and spotted hills, dry creek bottoms and circling buzzards. Now, as they neared the river where he and his parents were to make their home, the gullies were occasionally wet. Nothing else had changed. There wasn't a sign of human life.

Where are they? Elias thought. The Indians. The night before he'd stared at the ceiling, hoping to high heaven the tribes were as peaceful as his father believed. All the time he couldn't help remembering the terrifying stories of Comanches told by Corporal Higgins and the troopers, how naked savages ran down old ladies with spears and skinned children alive, then cooked them on spits like chickens.

"It's all nonsense, of course," Captain Rogers had declared when Elias asked about it. "There aren't any Comanches down at the agency. Caddos, sure, and Anadarkos, even a few Tonkawas. But the Comanches have their own agency, out west on the Clear Fork."

Tribal names didn't mean anything to Elias, though. He'd heard all about Indians from Timothy Phelps back in Waco. If they were so peaceful, why were Captain Rogers and a corporal's guard riding alongside as escort?

The left front wheel of the wagon struck a large rock, and Elias slammed against the side of his father's steamer trunk.

"You all right, son?" his father called from the front of the wagon.

"Fine, Papa," Elias said, rubbing his side and fighting to recover his breath.

"Not too much farther now, Elias. A mile or two maybe."

Elias nodded to his father, then wiped sweat from his forehead. Texas had always been hot, but out there in the open, with sandstone rocks radiating the sun's brightness, it was an inferno. He understood why the Indians rode bare-chested.

Elias glanced back at the equally uncomfortable soldiers. Captain Rogers rode as always, rigid, keeping his eyes on the trail and his mind on the business at hand. Slim, his graying hair and neatly trimmed moustache testifying to twenty years service on the frontier, the captain ignored the heat.

Alongside was Corporal Higgins, Higgy to the soldiers, a smallish Irishman whose stories of Indian fighting could curl your hair. The four privates, grumbling as they slouched in their saddles, completed the little guard. Elias didn't believe a one of them would stand and fight if Comanches appeared. More likely they would head in four different directions, whooping and hollering like that bunch from Mrs. Appleby's Girls Academy the time Tim Phelps dropped his hornet's nest down their chimney last February. As a reward for his part in the prank, Elias had slept on his belly that night. The other end had been too tender to touch so much as a feather bed.

"You'll have to restrain your devilish ways out here," his father had warned when telling Elias of the move to Belknap Agency. "These Indians expect a boy of thirteen to be more serious, to work in the manner of a man."

Elias shrugged his shoulders and ducked to avoid a wicked tree limb. Coming up from Trinity Crossing, he'd lost a half inch of shoulder to a locust tree. Some of those thorns were a full inch long!

I wish I'd stayed with Rebecca, he thought, staring at the hostile countryside again. For a week Elias had entertained the notion of staying in Waco with his sister and her husband. But in the end his mother objected.

"It's enough of a trial, Peter, going into the wilderness, leaving our friends behind, bidding farewell to Rebecca and her James, having Elizabeth in New Orleans and Joshua away in St. Louis. I won't say good-bye to all my children. And besides, Elias can help with the younger students. He's quick of mind, even if he fails to show it at times. He'll be of help."

So that was settled. Elias, like the trunks of clothing, the crates of pewter ware, and the bolts of cloth, had been piled into the wagon and headed west.

As they reached the crest of a small hill, Elias saw his first sign of life. Below them, huddled together along both banks of a small creek, were three wooden cabins. A cook fire sent a spiral of smoke skyward, and three or four women appeared to be grinding corn into meal using flat stones. Men tended rows of stunted corn in a nearby clearing. The children splashed along the creek. As the wagon grew nearer, Elias saw that the swimmers were stark naked.

"Oh, my," his mother said, turning away as the laughing boys and girls raced each other toward the wagon.

"Best get used to that, ma'am," Captain Rogers said, riding alongside and waving to the children. "Out here even the white boys disdain clothes. You'll be lucky to keep young Elias in so much as a shirt in the summer."

Elias turned crimson as his mother stared at him, and the soldiers laughed.

"This is the beginning of the Caddo encampments," Captain Rogers went on to say. "Indian Springs, they call the place. Most are between here and Dry Creek. The other tribes, what there is of them, scatter here and there, mostly along the river."

"And the . . . Comanches?" Elias asked.

Two of the Indian boys who were trotting alongside the wagon heard the question. They understood only the word *Comanche*, but it was enough to chase away their laughter.

"No Comanches," Captain Rogers quickly said, as much to the Caddos as to Elias. "Some are down at the other agency, on the Clear Fork of the Brazos. Others are still out on the Llano."

The Caddos, seemingly reassured, turned back to the creek, and Captain Rogers resumed his place behind the wagon.

"There's to be no more talk of Comanches," Elias's father told him. "We're in no danger here. Trust in what I say, Elias. I wouldn't bring your mama into danger, would I?"

"No, sir," Elias agreed.

"Nor you either, son. I know this place will prove a trial to you for a time, but you'll grow to feel as at home here on the Brazos as you did in Columbia or Waco."

"I'll miss my friends," Elias grumbled.

"I, too," his mother said. "But we'll make new ones, Elias. We always have. And think of the good work your father will do here, bringing knowledge to these Indians. You'll be a part of that."

Elias nodded, but he remained unconvinced. For the first time he'd be alone in the house. His brother Joshua was off to read the law with Uncle Henry in St. Louis, and their sisters were married and far away. From what Corporal Higgins had said, Elias gathered the only white people at the agency were Captain Rogers' family, an old farmer, and a blacksmith who split his time between the fort and the two Indian agencies.

The wagon splashed through the shallow water of the creek and continued toward the agency. The narrow trail began to widen, growing into a sandy path wide enough for two wagons to pass alongside. Soon houses of mesquite pickets appeared, and as they climbed a second ridge, Elias saw for the first time the churning waters of the Brazos as the river cut a canyon through the plain.

"We're here," Elias's father announced, pointing to a group of wooden buildings ahead. Elias heard his mother sigh, and he himself took a deep breath.

It can't be, he thought. A hundred yards from the river stood an undersized wooden cabin of unpainted oak planks. Nearby was something akin to a stable or small barn. Beyond that were two other structures, both apparently deserted. The only sign of life came from a fresh-faced young woman in her late teens, standing beside a picket cabin a quarter mile past.

"Papa!" the girl cried out as she ran to greet the soldiers.

Captain Rogers gave Corporal Higgins instructions for unloading the wagon, then dismounted and met the girl with outstretched arms.

"Alice, I'd like you to meet Mr. and Mrs. Walsh," the captain said, turning the girl's attention toward Elias's family. "That scruff of blond hair there in the back's their boy, Elias."

Elias nodded to the girl, and his mother complimented her on her reddish brown hair.

"This is my daughter Alice," Captain Rogers explained. "Since my dear wife's passing, Alice keeps house for me and tends to the agency paperwork."

"I helped Mr. Blanton teach the girls last spring," Alice said. "I speak a little Caddo, and being Papa's daughter, they trust me."

"I'd be grateful for any assistance you could offer me," Mr. Walsh said, climbing down from the wagon. "In addition, we'd be most pleased if you'd take supper with us when your father's away. My wife misses her own girls, and a pleasant face would be welcome."

"Thank you, sir," Alice said, smiling brightly. "I'd like that."

"Well, we'd best get this wagon unloaded," Captain Rogers said, removing the pins holding the back planks of the wagon in place. "Supplies to the schoolhouse, corporal. Everything else to the cabin."

"Yes, sir," Corporal Higgins answered, waving the soldiers off their horses. "We'll see to it."

"You might want to inspect the schoolhouse, Mr. Walsh," the captain said then, pointing to the smaller of the deserted structures. "It's been idle since Mr. Blanton left. We swept the house, and Alice cleaned it up some. But it's in need of a woman's touch, Mr. Blanton being unmarried and none too fine a housekeeper."

"I've got some cloth for curtains, Mrs. Walsh," Alice said, leading Elias's mother away.

"Papa," Elias said, holding onto his father's arm. "What am I to do?"

"Why don't you walk around a bit, acquaint yourself with the place," Captain Rogers suggested. "It can't have been a gentle ride in the back of that wagon. When your legs are themselves again, you might open up the barn, give the place some air."

"And afterward, split some wood for the stove, son," Mr. Walsh said. "But that can wait awhile. Just watch you don't let those hands of yours turn to mischief. There's too much work to be done to go pranking just yet."

"Yes, sir," Elias said, catching a hint of a glimmer in his father's eyes.

For better than an hour Elias explored the hillside above the river. A dozen odd white oaks towered above the rocky ground, and Elias rested beneath one of them for a time. A breeze eased the heat some, but Elias found himself envying the Caddos back at Indian Springs. He'd as soon shed his shirt and shoes, but his mother would hardly appreciate that, especially with Alice and Captain Rogers there.

Is this a punishment? Elias wondered as he swept his moist hair back from his forehead. His father had warned their life might be hard, that they must be prepared for the difficulties of the frontier. But that cabin! In Waco they'd had half a two-story house with a wide veranda. The room Elias had shared with his brother was as large as that whole cabin. And the school! Twin Oaks, the academy where Peter Walsh had taught French and geography, consisted of seven brick buildings neatly arranged around a grassy quadrangle.

Why'd you bring us here, Papa? Elias silently asked. A frown spread across the boy's face, and his usually bright blue eyes clouded over with despair. But for better or worse, the Walshes were there, and Elias knew his father would stay. ·

"A man can't back away from challenges," Peter Walsh was fond of saying. "The greatest pleasure in life is in making new discoveries, in testing yourself against the impossible. A mind can go to seed if it doesn't stretch itself."

"Couldn't we test ourselves in St. Louis, Papa?" Elias had asked. "Josh's there."

"I'm a teacher, son, and the test for a teacher is to seek out those who want to learn, help them along the path to knowledge."

Elias stared at the empty hillside and shook his head. These Indians didn't even know about wearing trousers. How can you teach someone to read when he doesn't speak your language? It was hopeless.

Elias stumbled to his feet and finally headed toward the barn. For his part, he'd do what he could, what he was told. He admired his father for trying, but it probably would come to nothing. Indians enjoyed riding horses and hunting buffalo, scalping women and little kids. And the ground seemed too rocky for corn.

Elias wiped away the sweat again and sighed. The barn would be like an oven, likely smelled of horse leavings, and he had no great urge to work there. The large doors facing toward the house were shut, seemingly bolted from inside. Another door opened from the rear, so Elias trudged back there and turned the doorknob. The door opened with a terrible screech, and three sparrows fluttered from their nest in the eaves overhead.

Better than hornets, Elias told himself. Then, knocking a cloud of cobwebs out of the way, he crept inside the barn and tried to adjust to the darkness. Hay was strewn about the floor, and a horse stood panting in one of the six stalls which lined the far wall. As light filtered inside through the open door, Elias discovered the place oddly fresh. Except for the cobwebs in the doorway, the barn appeared no different from an oft-used livery in Waco or Austin.

Something's wrong, Elias told himself. Unless the soldiers have been in here . . .

He had no time to complete his thought. Bright sunlight suddenly flooded the barn's interior as a window opened from the loft overhead. Elias shrank back from the brightness, and a figure appeared, jumping suddenly from the loft to the floor. There, bare-chested, naked save for a bit of buckskin about the waist, was a fierce-eyed, raven-haired . . . Indian!

2.

Elias stood frozen to the floor as the Indian examined him. Elias himself was too fearful to move a muscle. Pure terror filled every inch of his being. Finally, the Indian moved back a few feet and sat in the straw, gazing up into Elias's terrified face.

Now Elias began to calm a bit. So far the Indian had made no hostile moves. Elias remembered what Josh had told him about rattlesnakes. "Stay calm. Don't make any sudden movements. Show them you mean them no harm. And a smile wouldn't kill you."

Elias tried to grin, but his face wouldn't cooperate. He began to notice things about his mysterious companion. The Indian couldn't be much older than Elias himself, maybe fourteen, certainly no older than sixteen. Long dark hair fell onto the Indian's bronze shoulders. His dark eyes blazed with intensity, and his stone face hinted of danger. Three fingerlike scars marked his left side, just below the ribs. Another scar crossed the right knee.

"I . . . I, uh, I . . ." Elias tried to say. But his lips quivered, and the Indian seemed not to understand anyway. So Elias searched his memory for some of the signs the soldiers at Fort Belknap had explained could be used for speaking to Comanches.

"I don't remember," Elias said, slapping the side of his leg. The sudden movement brought a scowl to the Indian's face, and Elias felt his knees wobble. He was close to desperation.

"I, uh," he began again. "No, me, uh . . . me friend," Elias finally managed. "Friend," he repeated, pounding a finger into his chest. "No harm you. Me come to help teach Indian. Good."

The Indian seemed not to understand, and Elias repeated his words more slowly, making exaggerated movements to illustrate his meaning.

"Me . . . no . . . harm . . . you. Understand? You . . . no . . . harm . . . me?"

Finally the Indian boy reached behind his back, and Elias shuddered. Oh, no, he thought. This is it. He's got a knife, and he's going to murder me. But instead the Indian produced a small envelope. Inside was a letter carefully written in ink by Major Neighbors, agent for the Texas tribes.

Elias only half digested the words. There was a welcome to the Brazos, a few sentences of general information, something about chickens, and the mention of an interpreter.

"You're not a Comanche?" Elias finally asked.

"Comanche?" the Indian asked. "No. Tonkawa. I'm called Thomas Three Feathers."

"You speak English?"

"Yes," Thomas said matter-of-factly. "Major Neighbors sent me to help you. I also speak some Caddo words, enough to be understood."

"You speak English," Elias mumbled. "You speak English, and you let me jabber away like an idiot?"

"My father taught me never to interrupt."

"Your father?"

"He is called Joseph Three Feathers. Of course, the whites named him Joseph. Three Feathers is his Tonkawa name. He is a scout for the soldiers down south at Fort Mason."

"Did you learn English from the soldiers?"

Thomas nodded, then stepped toward the horse.

"How long have you been here?" Elias asked, joining Thomas beside the stall.

"Three days. Miss Alice said I could sleep here. I cleaned the barn. It was not a fit place for horses when I arrived. The old teacher had no horse. The Caddos didn't like him. How can a man without a horse teach Indians?"

"My father loves horses," Elias said, lightly touching the flank of Thomas's pony. "Our wagon is pulled by mules, though. They're not so good for riding."

"Hard on the—"

"Bottom," Elias said, sharing the thought. "I've heard Indians ride without saddles. Do you?"

"Sometimes," Thomas said, stroking his horse's nose. "My father says I ride like a white man, though. With saddle or without."

"I don't understand."

"He means I am too . . . too . . ." Thomas scratched his head, searching for the word. Finally he put the fingers of his left hand together and held them rigidly still.

"Too straight," Elias said. "Too stiff."

"Yes," Thomas said, smiling. "A Tonkawa rides his horse close to the neck, low so his enemy can't see him. I've been at Fort Mason too long. Soon I'll forget everything."

Elias laughed, but Thomas's eyes burned fiercely. It was clear the young Tonkawa was worried by the thought.

"Come, Thomas, I'll take you to my father," Elias said, motioning toward the bolted doors of the barn.

"Your father is the teacher?"

"Yes," Elias said proudly. "Peter Walsh."

"Wal-ush?" Thomas said. "It means something?"

"Maybe once. Now it's just a name."

"And you?"

"I guess I ought to grow a brain, eh?" Elias asked, laughing. "Elias."

"Eee-li-us?"

"I don't know that it means anything, either, but it was my grandfather's name. He was a sailor."

"Sailor?"

"Went to sea. Hunted whales."

"Whales?"

"I'll explain later," Elias promised. "Now I'll take you to Papa."

Elias started toward the door, but Thomas pulled him back.

"Can you help me?" Thomas asked, pointing to several small bundles wrapped in brown paper.

"Your things?" Elias asked. "You want to take them to the house?"

"Not for me," Thomas said, shaking his head. "Presents. For the teacher."

"From Major Neighbors?" Elias asked.

"From my father," Thomas said, his eyes blazing. "To welcome him as a friend."

"I'll help you," Elias said, accepting three of the packages in his arms, then waiting while Thomas took the rest. They walked together to the schoolhouse.

"Papa?" Elias called out. "Papa?"

Peter Walsh appeared in the door, put aside his broom, and greeted the boys.

"This is Thomas Three Feathers," Elias explained. "He's a Tonkawa, and he speaks good English. He has a letter and some presents for you."

"Oh?" Mr. Walsh asked.

Thomas handed over the letter, then began unwrapping the bundles while Mr. Walsh read the contents.

"You're my interpreter?" Mr. Walsh asked nervously. "You're very young. Do you speak the languages of the other tribes?"

"I'm fourteen," Thomas declared. "From the time I first spoke, I have lived among the Caddos and Anadarkos. I also know the Wichitas."

"It says I'm to teach you to read and write. You've had no schooling?"

"Indians don't go to school at Fort Mason," Thomas said, trembling slightly. "My father says it is important to understand the marks on the papers. I will learn so that I can teach others."

"It's not so hard," Elias said. "If I can learn, you can."

"So long as you work harder at it than Elias does," Mr. Walsh said, laughing.

"I work hard," Thomas said, stone-faced as before. "I will learn."

Thomas then presented his gifts. There were six parcels in all: two pairs of moccasins, an old flint knife, a shirt of buckskin painted with Tonkawa symbols, and two beaded pouches.

"There is a story to each, but I will save that for another time," Thomas said. "There is work to do now."

"Yes, there is," Mr. Walsh agreed. "Elias, the mules should be fed and watered, and the wagon needs to be put inside the barn. Some Indians are bringing two crates of chickens for the coop, and your mama will be wanting some wood split for the stove. If you want dinner, that is."

"I do," Elias said, grinning.

"Then be about it, son," Mr. Walsh said, clapping his hands. "Don't dawdle."

"No, sir," Elias said, motioning for Thomas to follow toward the barn.

The two of them unhitched the mules and led each to a stall inside the barn. Next they rolled the wagon inside.

"Is there a pump?" Elias asked, glancing around in hope of spotting one. Thomas pointed to the river, and

Elias nodded. They grabbed pails and began the tiresome chore of fetching water for the animals. Actually the river was less than a hundred yards distant, but lugging pails of water to the barn grew tedious quickly. Afterward, oats were placed in the feed troughs for the animals, and Elias slumped to the floor.

"My brother Joshua used to tend the animals," Elias explained. "He's older by six years. Now he's in St. Louis, reading for the law. I have two sisters, too. They're married."

Thomas appeared a bit uneasy as Elias spoke of aunts and uncles, cousins in a dozen different places.

"Well?" Elias finally asked. "What do you know?"

"You like to talk," Thomas said, grinning.

"I do, don't I?" Elias said, laughing at himself. "Well, I guess everybody's entitled to one vice. Or two or three. Guess we better see the chickens get put inside the coop."

Thomas nodded, and the two of them walked to the chicken coop. The Indians had already installed the birds in their home, though, carefully latching the door to prevent escape.

"Then I guess it's time to split logs," Elias said, sighing.

Thomas again demonstrated his value. Elias, chop as he might, always required at least three blows to drive the wedge through the log and split it in two. Thomas raised the big two-bitted ax over his powerful shoulders and sent it crashing downward with terrifying force. Often as not, the log was cleft into pieces.

I guess it helps to be born to this kind of life, Elias thought as he collected the splinters of wood and carried them to his mother's kindling box. He envied Thomas his strength, the ease with which he made the most difficult task appear simple.

"You finished that job quickly enough," Mrs. Walsh declared when Elias dropped the final load into the box. "Now wash up for supper."

"Yes, ma'am," Elias answered.

"Elias, tell your young friend we wear trousers here to dinner. And shirts."

"It's awful hot, Mama," Elias said, touching his own sweat-streaked cotton shirt.

"Thomas is here to learn civilized ways," she said. "We can't let ourselves forget that, Lias."

"Sure," Elias said, surrendering to her will. "I'll get washed up."

Thomas was none too happy to tote more water to the house, and he was even less happy to learn Mrs. Walsh's other instructions.

"I'm not a white man," Thomas declared on the way back to the barn.

"Sometimes I wish I wasn't," Elias grumbled. "It doesn't matter, though. Mama never backs down once she makes up her mind. She's more stubborn than a mule. We'd best clean up and get dressed."

They splashed off the worst of their weariness with the water, then brushed back their hair. Thomas exchanged his breechclout for a pair of cotton trousers. But as Elias buttoned his collar, Thomas sat sadly beside his horse and stared off toward the river.

"What's wrong?" Elias asked. "Miss your family?"

"Nothing's wrong," Thomas said, turning away.

"Of course not. That's why you're staring at the tail end of that horse. Am I that ugly?"

Thomas half smiled, and Elias broke into a broad grin.

"See, I'm not bad company for a skinny white boy," Elias said, laughing. "What's the trouble?"

"I don't have a shirt," Thomas whispered, shifting his feet nervously.

"I've got a couple of Josh's old ones in my trunk up at the house. I'll get one. They'll fit you better'n one of mine."

Thomas nodded, and Elias scrambled out of the barn and on to the house. Moments later he returned with a blue poplin shirt, and Thomas slipped it over his shoulders.

"It's a little big," Elias observed, "but it'll do. Mama might make you some. We've got lots of material."

Thomas appeared uncomfortable at the notion, but Elias shook it off.

"A present for you, just like the ones you brought. Understand?"

Thomas nodded, and they walked together to the house.

Dinner was strange, to say the least. Captain Rogers had brought along some fresh meat, and Mrs. Walsh had roasted a large piece together with potatoes and carrots. The captain and Alice joined Thomas and the Walshes in the confines of the cabin's single chamber, and there was barely space to breathe.

But the crowded room was only to be expected. Thomas's curiosity was not. The vegetables were largely foreign, and he wanted to know all about them. How they could be grown, and how they should be cooked.

| 19

Elias was confused. He couldn't imagine anything more common than a carrot or a potato. But Captain Rogers insisted vegetables were a rare treat on the frontier. Onions and turnips grew wild, as did other greens. But only where gardens were tended could a carrot or a pea be found.

"He finds our ways strange," Elias's father told him afterward. "You'll judge his customs just as odd. The Caddos think nothing of running about near naked, but you'd turn red as a tomato if your mama or Alice caught a glimpse of you bare-bottomed in a river. The Tonkawas eat roots and herbs you've never seen before. They're just as odd to you as a carrot is to Thomas. You two will learn from each other."

"Yes, sir," Elias agreed.

"Now, son, I've got something to ask you. A favor, so to speak."

"Sir?"

"This little cabin of ours was built for a single man. There's but the one bed. Later we'll add a room for you. Just now I'd like—"

"You want me to sleep in the barn with Thomas, don't you?" Elias asked, shaking slightly. "With the mules and all?"

"If you'd rather, we can stuff a mattress for you and place it in the schoolhouse."

"But you want me to share the barn with Thomas."

"You'd be able to watch the stock that way, too."

"Papa . . ."

"I know it's strange for you here, Lias, and this isn't going to help. But Thomas is alone here. You remember how you felt the night after Joshua left for St. Louis? Some company would be nice, don't you think?"

"Yes, sir," Elias admitted. "I'd better fetch my trunk over."

"Need some help?"

"I can manage it, Papa. Good night."

"Good night, son," Mr. Walsh said, touching Elias on the head lightly, then stroking the boy's shoulder. "Remember, morning comes early."

"Yes, sir."

Elias dragged his trunk to the barn. Thomas lay atop a coarse woolen blanket, his lower half covered by a sheet of cotton cloth.

"I'm to share the barn with you," Elias explained, stuffing a mattress with hay and tossing it against the wall of the barn a few feet from the Tonkawa's blankets. "All right with you?"

Thomas shrugged, then grinned as Elias slipped out of his clothes.

"What's so funny?" Elias asked.

"I never saw anyone so white," Thomas said, fighting to keep a straight face. "Not even the soldiers."

"I get a little darker before summer ends."

"What is that?" Thomas asked as Elias shed his trousers and wriggled into his long yellow nightshirt.

"It's a nightshirt. For sleeping. Back in Waco, it's considered indecent to sleep naked."

"Waco? I know of the Waco tribe."

"Waco is a town. A big one, with many buildings."

"This isn't Waco," Thomas said, shaking his head. "You'll learn. In summer heat, bare is best."

Elias thought it likely, but he also knew his mother would scream to high heaven if she found him shirtless in the morning.

"It's quiet tonight," Elias said as darkness settled in around them.

"No, the night just has different sounds," Thomas said. "I hear the frogs at the river's edge. There are crickets, too. And I hear the owl in the hollow oak outside. He hunts mice for his dinner."

"I don't hear—"

"Be quiet. Listen. You must have ears for their sounds."

Elias lay still. After a few moments the chirping of the crickets and the croaking of the frogs became distinct sounds. He heard the owl, as well as the sparrows in the eaves. Finally he heard something else, a distant howling that brought shivers down his spine.

"What's that?" Elias asked, sitting up.

"The wolf," Thomas told him. "Howling at the moon, as he always has. It's said the wolf was born of the moon, and he calls for his lost mother."

"A wolf?" Elias asked nervously.

"I saw one as I rode here, a large gray wolf with dark eyes. He hunts his dinner as the owl does, by night when his enemies can't see. The wolf is cunning and brave. He hunts in darkness, coming upon his prey and striking swiftly as the eagle."

Elias shuddered at the thought. And later, when Thomas was fast asleep, Elias heard the wolf again. Other noises crept through his mind, the screams of Comanches and the growls of cougars, all come to taste the soft white flesh of Elias Walsh.

"Thomas?" Elias whispered, hoping his companion would stir. But Thomas slept on, and Elias suffered the terrifying silence and the frightening sounds of movement through the grasses outside the barn alone.

3.

As Elias's father had promised, morning arrived early. A rooster crowed loudly at the first hint of the sun, and Elias shook himself awake. He'd managed only a little sleep that night, and his eyes were as red as the morning horizon. As he shed his nightshirt and pulled on his clothes, he discovered Thomas had vanished.

"Thomas?" Elias called out, searching the barn for some trace of the young Tonkawa. "Thomas?"

No one replied, so Elias saw to it that the animals still had water, then walked out the twin doors of the barn into the morning mist. Even in the dim light, he could tell something was wrong. Small white feathers were scattered across the ground between the barn and the chicken coop, and Elias recalled the noises he'd heard the night before. A chill crept up his spine, and he stepped back. Only when he located Thomas kneeling beside the coop did Elias relax.

"What happened?" Elias asked, slowly, cautiously continuing toward the coop.

Thomas pointed first to the splintered planks on the side of the coop, then to large footprints in the nearby earth.

"What was it?" Elias asked, studying the prints. "Not dogs?"

"It was the wolf you heard," Thomas explained. "And others."

"I thought I heard something outside last night."

"I count three gone. We must tell your father."

"I'd better do it," Elias said, glancing at his feet. Thomas nodded, and Elias reluctantly trudged on toward the house. He could smell the fire burning in the stove, and as he opened the door, his mother met him with a smile.

"I'm glad you're up and about at last," she said. "Gather the eggs, will you, Elias? And rouse Thomas."

"He's roused," Elias said, frowning. "Mama, I'll get the eggs, but Papa best know. A wolf got at the chickens."

"What?"

"A wolf took three of the chickens. Tore up the coop, too."

"Go fetch the eggs, Lias," his mother said. "I'll tell your papa. Not the best of beginnings, is it?"

"No, ma'am," Elias agreed as he started out the door.

By the time he'd collected those eggs not broken in the commotion of the night before, his father had arrived to inspect the damage.

"We only had a dozen birds to start with," Mr. Walsh

complained. "Now three are dead, and I've got half a day's work ahead just repairing the coop."

"We can do that," Elias said, motioning to Thomas.

"It's wasted effort anyway," Elias's father said, placing his hands on his hips. "The wolves will come back. Do you know how long it takes to bring supplies down here from Fort Belknap? Not to mention getting them to the fort. What's next?"

"Wolves have always been here," Thomas said, joining them. "They hunt the rabbit and the quail. Now they see chickens trapped in this coop. You must make it hard for them, not easy."

"How?" Elias asked.

"Make the coop stronger. Set out traps."

"We've got some heavy planking," Mr. Walsh said. "We can strengthen the sides. But I have no traps."

"We can make them," Thomas explained. "But the best way is to hunt the wolves."

"Papa?" Elias asked.

"No," Mr. Walsh said, frowning. "It's too dangerous. Besides, we've got a year's work to do before the children arrive next week for the beginning of school. But I've got a shotgun in the house. I'll bring it out to the barn tonight. If you hear something, fire off a shot."

"Yes, sir," Elias said.

"That will likely scare even a wolf away," Mr. Walsh said, patting Elias lightly on the back. "I don't want you trying to fight them off or anything of the like, boys. Night is the realm of the wolf, and you're not to tempt fate by doing battle on his terms. Understand?"

"Yes, sir," Elias said for the both of them.

"Now, let's take those eggs to your mother, Elias. After breakfast, we can get back to work."

Work was exactly what they got back to. In addition to repairing the coop, there were a hundred other tasks to be done. Elias spent most of the day helping his father split juniper logs into shingles. Thomas devoted himself to setting snares out in the path of the wolves.

"Don't you think Thomas might need some help, Papa?" Elias asked in midafternoon.

"Leave Thomas to do what he knows best," Mr. Walsh declared. "I need you up here on this roof."

Elias sighed and continued. The roof felt like the inside of his mother's stove, and he noticed both he and his father were growing red about the face and ears. Elias couldn't help envying Thomas, working in the shade of the white oaks and junipers off where the wind blew cool and refreshing from the river.

The two days that followed were no different. The shingles were finished, and the roof of the house would keep out the rain. But whole planks were missing from the school walls, and the students would need benches and tables on which to work. All the buildings required paint, and even the dozen soldiers sent by Major Neighbors could not complete all the tasks.

While Elias hammered and painted, Thomas tended the animals or disappeared downriver where the Caddo boys busied themselves swimming and fishing. The catfish Thomas brought Elias's mother were a welcome change from dried beef and salt pork, but the thought of Thomas splashing away the afternoon heat in the cool of the river did little to lift Elias's spirits.

"I don't see why he can't help more with readying the school," Elias complained to Alice Rogers. "Learning to paint's not hard. After all, the school's for *his* people."

"You don't understand, Elias," she told him.

"I understand he's lazy."

"Is that what you truly think?" she asked. "If you do, you're wrong. These Indians have been going to school all their lives. Not in a classroom, but out there in the hills, among the trees and the animals. Thomas wouldn't understand why your father needs a building to teach. He hasn't said anything because he respects our right to do things our way. But to him, it must seem crazy to work so hard for something so totally unimportant."

"He thinks Papa ought to have his school out here in the open?"

"It would be cooler."

Elias shook his head and sighed.

"I don't see how we're ever going to get along, Alice. I don't ever know what he's thinking, and he almost never says what he feels."

"It's hard," she said, nodding to show she understood. "But I've always found the secret to treating with Indians, especially the tribes here like the Caddo and the Tonkawa, is to be honest. Explain yourself. Let them know when you're pleased, and when you're not. Sincerity and courage are respected. And don't forget—Thomas is all alone here. He'll need a friend."

Elias nodded. I will, too, he thought, looking around at the sunbaked land that was so different from the towns and cities he knew.

The arrival of Sunday brought the first break in a week of almost constant toil. As Elias washed for breakfast, he rubbed his aching shoulders and frowned at his sunburned face and neck. After bringing fresh water to the animals and filling the barrel in the kitchen, Elias sat at the table with his parents and Thomas and enjoyed the first breakfast since leaving Waco that wasn't the beginning of a difficult day's labors.

"For us, Sunday is a time of rest," Elias explained to Thomas as they walked from the house to the barn. "Papa will read verses from his Bible tonight after supper. The rest of the day is ours to enjoy."

Thomas shook his head in dismay. Elias decided it must seem a bit crazy to the Indians. After all, Thomas had been enjoying every day.

"Would you like to come with me to the river?" Thomas asked as he unbuttoned his shirt. "It's cool there."

"Sure," Elias said, slipping out of his shoes.

"Good," Thomas declared, exchanging his trousers for the breechclout he preferred. "I was worried about you."

"Worried?" Elias asked, checking to make sure his mother was inside as he peeled off his shirt.

"You are too white," Thomas explained, touching Elias's side. "Look too much like a chicken. I wouldn't want the wolves to eat you."

Elias scowled, but Thomas laughed for the first time in days. Then Thomas grabbed Elias's hand and led the way out the back door of the barn and on toward the river.

By the time they arrived at the Brazos, four young Caddos were already splashing away in the shallows. Thomas spoke to them, mentioned Elias by name, and all four yelled a greeting.

"These are my friends, the Caddos," Thomas explained. "The small one is Andrew Riversnake. There beside the rocks is Austin Crowheart. The others are Sam Jackson and little Joseph, his brother."

"Hello," Elias said, and the Caddos answered him, "Chel-lo." All four grinned, and Elias smiled back. Then Thomas removed his clothes and dove into the water. Elias rolled up his trouser legs and waded into the shallows. The others stared at him, and Sam Jackson asked Thomas something.

"He wants to know if white men always wear their pants?" Thomas said, laughing. "You don't swim like that, do you?"

"I don't swim at all," Elias explained. "I don't know how."

Thomas told the others, and all five laughed.

"I will teach you," Thomas offered. "But you must come out a little deeper."

"I don't know," Elias said nervously. "I can't swim at all. You understand?"

"I taught my brothers," Thomas said, coming to Elias's side and taking his hand.

"Wait," Elias said as the Caddos began slapping the water and crying out encouragement. "I guess I better get out of my trousers."

Thomas nodded, and Elias retreated to the safety of the shore. But when he made no effort to return to the river, Thomas and the others raced to his side, helped him out of his clothes, and dragged him back to the river.

"No!" Elias screamed as they threw him into the river. "I can't swim!"

Elias frantically kicked and slapped at the water, but it was hopeless. His mouth filled with water, and he coughed for air. He could feel himself slip beneath the surface. Finally Thomas grabbed his shoulders and steadied him. Soon Elias found himself standing, water reaching just up to his shoulders. The river wasn't really very deep there.

"You won't drown," Thomas said, leading the way into deeper water. "I will show you how to swim. It's easy."

But in spite of Thomas's advice and the occasional cheers of the young Caddos, Elias managed to spend more time under the surface than atop it.

"You will learn in time," Thomas said when they sat together beneath a white oak and shook themselves dry.

The Caddos called out to them to return, but Elias shook his head, and Thomas waved them off.

"You have earned a name today, Elias," Thomas said, smiling with approval.

"A name?"

"Indian boys must earn their names. I am called Younger Raven because my mother's brother was called Raven. I followed him often when I lived in his lodge."

"So what am I called?"

"White Bottom," Thomas said, pointing to Elias's bare rear. "It's all we could see when you tried to swim."

"Just don't tell Mama," Elias pleaded. "If she finds out I was running around out here naked, she'd turn my bottom red as a tomato."

Thomas didn't seem to understand, but Elias's smile was enough of an explanation. And after an hour of rest,

Thomas persuaded Elias to take another try at swimming. Elias managed to stay afloat for a full minute before sinking this time.

Learning to swim was nothing compared to the trial Elias faced before supper, though. The Walshes dressed for Sunday supper, and Elias had great difficulty convincing Thomas a necktie wasn't some white man's torture that should be reserved for Comanche captives.

"I wear a shirt to please your mother, but I will not put this thing around my neck!" Thomas declared. "I can't breathe."

"It's not so bad, and it's only until Papa finishes his Bible reading after supper."

Thomas finally nodded, but he only managed to convert the necktie into a jumble of knots.

"I'll never make it look like yours," Thomas said, throwing the tie to the floor. "A Tonkawa shouldn't be made into a white man."

"It's just one day a week," Elias told him. "Besides, it's better than learning to swim. I'll show you how. It's pretty easy."

Thomas was unconvinced, but Elias got a knot formed. Thomas gagged, but Elias only laughed.

"It's too hot," Thomas complained as Elias passed over a jacket.

"It's that or no supper," Elias explained. "And Mama baked biscuits."

Thomas frowned. By now he'd learned to appreciate Mrs. Walsh's talents in the kitchen.

"I always thought it was easy to be a white man,"

Thomas whispered as they walked to the house. "I was wrong."

Elias laughed, and at that moment, their friendship was sealed.

4.

That night Elias quickly fell into a sound sleep. But a little short of midnight he was awakened by something stirring in the brush behind the barn. He blinked himself awake, then sat up. Ten feet away Thomas was quietly dressing.

Outside, a terrible whine disturbed the quiet of the night. In answer a howl came from farther away. As Elias scrambled into his clothes, he heard the chickens stirring in the coop, flapping their useless wings and cackling in alarm.

"Wait for me," Elias whispered as Thomas started toward the door. Thomas hesitated, and Elias headed for the shelf where his father had set the shotgun, fastening the buttons on his shirt as he went.

"You can shoot that?" Thomas asked while Elias slid

two shells into the shotgun, then fixed the percussion caps into place. "Shotguns can be very dangerous."

"I've fired it before," Elias said, not bothering to explain it'd been in broad daylight or that the recoil had nearly torn his shoulder from his body.

"Remember who is the wolf. I am Thomas Three Feathers," Thomas said, tapping his chest.

"I know the difference between an Indian and a wolf," Elias said as he filled one pocket with extra caps and shells. "I won't shoot you."

As they made their way past the door of the barn, Elias stared into the darkness. The moon drifted in and out of a dark cloud, and it was difficult to locate the chicken coop, much less any wolf that might be lurking nearby.

"We'd best wake Papa," Elias declared.

"No Tonkawa would run to his father."

The words stung Elias, and he bit his lip. "Maybe we can build a fire, chase them away," he suggested.

"They would only come back," Thomas said, holding Elias in place. "A wolf must be fought. You heard the one crying in the woods? He has fallen into my trap. The others will be close by. We will kill them."

"What if they don't want to be killed?" Elias asked, trembling as the nightmare of jagged teeth and sharp claws reappeared in his mind. "What if . . ."

"Shhh," Thomas pleaded. "They are very near."

Elias shuddered. He could see nothing, but he trusted Thomas's ears. He watched carefully for the slightest hint of movement. But there was nothing.

"Thomas?" Elias whispered.

The young Tonkawa pointed to their right, and Elias cradled the heavy shotgun and followed his friend into the darkness.

"Shouldn't we stay with the chickens?" Elias asked.

"Wolves are hunters," Thomas said quietly. "They won't expect us to come in search of them."

I guess not, Elias thought as they made their way through the underbrush. No intelligent person would. His hands sweated, and the gun grew heavy. But he followed along anyway, searching for some sign of the wolves. Soon they reached the first of Thomas's traps.

"It was here," Thomas said, picking up a twig from the shattered trap. The snare had been chewed through, and part of it was covered with a warm, sticky liquid. Blood.

"Papa always says a wounded animal is the most dangerous kind," Elias whispered, shivering at the thought.

"Yes," Thomas agreed. "Come. We must find it."

Thomas led the way to a rocky clearing, then pointed to the left. Elias swung the barrel of the shotgun in that direction. The moon broke through the clouds, and he saw for the first time a deadly pair of green eyes glaring out from the far side of the clearing.

"There!" Thomas shouted as the wolf charged forward.

Elias struggled to raise the barrel, then pulled the right trigger. A terrific blast sent him reeling backward. As he struck the ground, the second barrel went off, driving the stock into the small of his shoulder.

Powder smoke stung his eyes and clouded the scene. The wolf uttered a single whimper, then grew silent.

"Ayyyy!" Thomas screamed, slapping Elias on the back. But no sooner had thoughts of triumph entered Elias's mind than they were chased away by a terrible growl. Turning quickly, Elias had but a glimpse of the second wolf before the animal hit him full force below the knees.

"Thomas!" Elias screamed as he felt himself roll away. Then the wolf sank its deadly teeth into his left leg, and he cried out in pain.

Elias wasn't entirely sure what happened next. He recalled thrashing out with his hands at the wolf, slamming a rock against the demon's nose. But pain exploded through his leg, and he saw nothing clearly. The wolf tore at his leg again, and Elias's face contorted in agony. He'd never known such pain in all his thirteen years. He fainted, and for a few seconds he felt nothing. But Thomas shook him back to life, and Elias clutched his leg with both hands and cried out.

"I can't feel my leg," Elias cried. "Is it still there?"

"Yes, and so is that wolf," Thomas whispered, tearing Elias's shirt from his chest and shredding it into bandages. "It's not so bad."

"Oh, no, just close to torn off," Elias cried, reaching out for the shotgun. Twenty feet away the wolf uttered a low growl.

"Can you load the shotgun?" Thomas asked as he bound the wounded leg.

"I think so," Elias said as he blinked away tears of pain. He fumbled with the shells, then drew two out of his pocket and slipped them into their chambers. Then he fixed the caps and readied himself for another charge by the wolf.

"You killed the first," Thomas said as he pulled the binding tight. "There's little left to be seen. I've seen it before with shotguns. Hard to miss so close."

"Yes," Elias said, trying to ward off the pain long enough to smile. "My Uncle Henry once shot a skunk. Smelled up half the county."

Thomas laughed nervously, and the fear returned to Elias.

"You've killed a wolf, Elias," Thomas said, stretching out beside Elias. "Wolfkiller, your name will now be."

"Better than White Bottom," Elias said, moaning as his leg throbbed. "I guess you've killed lots of wolves, being an Indian."

"Never," Thomas said. "A buffalo once with my bow. I was with Raven."

"Your uncle?"

"Yes, my mother's brother. But that was long ago, before I lived at the fort with my father. Sometimes my father took me to hunt the whitetail, but wolves don't bother hunters."

"Why doesn't it attack?" Elias asked, wincing as he adjusted the shotgun.

"Wolves hunt in packs. Maybe he waits on the others. One is dead. Maybe he will never come. He seeks food, not death. A chicken makes a good supper, but there is little meat on you."

Thomas touched Elias's ribs and laughed. The fear had left the young Tonkawa's voice, and Elias warmed.

"Maybe we should go back?" Elias asked.

"Soon," Thomas said, pulling a knife Elias had not seen. "Soon."

Thomas stood up and screamed a dozen Tonkawa words into the darkness. A wolf howled, and another raced through the brush. From the rocks a third darted forward, and Thomas yelled to fire. Elias closed his eyes and pulled back both triggers. The blast shook the ground and knocked Elias backward. But the charging wolf was blown apart, and the remaining animals whined and scurried back through a tangle of underbrush.

"Now we go back," Thomas announced, taking the shotgun in one hand and helping Elias up with the other. "Two Wolves, you have named yourself."

"Two Wolves," Elias mumbled as he leaned against the rock-hard side of his friend.

"It's not far," Thomas reminded Elias. "We'll be there quickly."

Elias took a step, then felt his injured leg grow numb. Thomas dragged him a few feet, then set down the shotgun and lifted Elias in his strong arms. The trees and the moon grew hazy then, and darkness clouded his mind.

Elias woke to find himself lying in his father's bed inside the cabin. A deep bruise spread across his shoulder, and his left trouser leg was shredded above the knee. Clean white bandages wrapped his thigh and shin, stained here and there where the bleeding had resumed.

"Mama?" Elias called out.

His mother turned away from the stove and hurried to his side.

"Lias, how do you feel?" she asked, taking his hands and pressing them tightly.

"Dizzy," he said, blinking the fog from his eyes. "My leg. A wolf . . ."

"Thomas carried you in last night. We heard shots. I thought Comanches were attacking. Your papa took his rifle and set out after you. Thomas brought you back, though. You could have been killed, Lias. What was in your mind, taking out after a pack of wolves in the darkness?"

"They were after the chickens," Elias said, groaning as he felt his leg throb. "Chickens came all the way from the fort. We can't let the wolves . . ."

"Hush now," she said, setting a wet cloth on his forehead. "Rest awhile. It's nearly noon. Your papa'll be coming by to see you."

"Papa? Where's Papa?"

"He's started the school, Lias. Thomas is there, too. That boy was concerned about you. I couldn't understand a word of what he was saying, but I could tell he was worried. He did a fine job binding your wounds, though. I'd say he's had practice."

Elias's mother continued talking, but he soon lost his ability to listen. His thoughts were whirling around in a hundred directions, remembering the wolves, dreaming of hunting buffalo with Thomas's uncle, feeling again the teeth of the wolf in his leg and crying out.

"You're safe now," his mother said, stroking Elias's hair. "It's only the fever. Once it breaks, you'll be your old self again."

"Fever?" Elias asked, fighting to keep his eyes open.

"Only the fever," his mother repeated.

I'll be all right, Elias told himself, smiling as he faded away. It's only the fever. His mother's words rolled around inside his head over and over until nothing remained, and he was swept away into a world of cold silence.

5.

When he next awoke, Elias found himself alone. Through the open window he could see the sky was darkening. He thought to rise from the bed, but the instant he moved his injured leg, pain shot up his spine, and he winced. Just as he'd begun to think himself deserted, though, there was a gentle knock on the outside wall of the cabin, and Alice Rogers stuck her head through the doorway.

"I see you're awake," she said, smiling. "I thought you might enjoy an orange. My father brought some back from the fort."

"Thanks," Elias said, taking the fruit from her and motioning toward the stool his mother had set beside the bed.

"I would have warned you that wolves bite, but I didn't

imagine you'd have the opportunity to find out," Alice said, helping him peel the orange.

"I've done smarter things in my life," Elias admitted.

"Still, you've become a sort of hero among the Indian boys. Two Wolves, Thomas calls you."

"I'd be more help to Papa if I'd stayed in bed. How's the school coming along?"

"Fair, I'd say. The little ones seem willing to learn, even eager. It's the older ones that are the challenge. They'd rather be out hunting. Learning to read's difficult enough when it's not a foreign tongue as well. But I imagine after a time they'll all settle down to the task."

Elias nodded, then broke apart the now peeled orange and placed a wedge of it in his mouth. He'd almost forgotten what one tasted like. Oranges were uncommon rare even in Waco. He offered Alice a piece, but she shook her head.

"For you," she told him. "Is the leg still tender?"

"It feels like it's got a couple of knives in there."

"Father says the post surgeon will come down tomorrow to have a look. He's not a real doctor, just an artillery captain with some training. But he's seen his share of frontier wounds."

"Mama's uncle was a doctor. She used to help him, so I know it'll heal up in time. I just hate to be flat on my back when there's so much that needs to be done."

"I wouldn't worry," Alice said, laughing. "Most of the Caddos who sent their children to the school have helped. Andrew Jackson is a good carpenter. He braced the benches. And I helped your mother with the curtains."

"How does an Indian get a name like Andrew Jackson?" Elias asked.

"Oh, the agents gave them names. Or soldiers did. Most of the Indian names are too hard to pronounce. There's a Sam Houston, a Stephen Austin, a James Polk, even a Daniel Webster."

"Thomas translated his Tonkawa name into English."

"Yes. Some of the others did, too. Of course, Thomas isn't really an agency Indian."

"He's not?"

"No. His father scouts for the army. I remember him when Father was stationed at Fort Mason. Thomas used to be kind of an unofficial private, a junior orderly of sorts."

"I thought he lived with his mother's brother."

"Not then," Alice said, scratching her head. "In fact, I don't recall his ever mentioning his mother to me. I just assumed something happened to her."

"Something happened to her? What?" Elias asked.

"I wouldn't know," Alice said, shrugging her shoulders. "I always figured she was dead."

Elias frowned. Thomas had never hinted at anything like that. But then Thomas didn't talk a lot about himself.

"It's time I was on my way," Alice finally said. "Your mother will be in with the washing soon, and I've supper to make for Father."

"Thanks again for the orange," Elias said as Alice turned away. Alice nodded, then continued on outside.

Elias expected his mother to appear shortly. It was well into afternoon, and she always liked to start supper early. But when someone did appear at the door, it wasn't Mrs.

Walsh. Instead Elias found himself staring into the bright eyes of Thomas Three Feathers.

"How does your leg feel?" Thomas asked.

"Like somebody sliced it open with an ax," Elias said, sitting up in spite of the pain. Thomas shrank back, the smile fading from his face. But Elias pointed to the stool.

"I meant to fight the wolf myself," Thomas said, reluctantly sitting down.

"I had the gun," Elias said, forcing a grin onto his face. "And I really didn't intend to get myself chewed on, either."

"The wound was deep, but it bled well."

"Bled well?"

"Sometimes the blood is dark, and there is an evil smell to it. I've seen legs fill with bad blood until they steal a man's life."

"It hurts some," Elias said, running his fingers along the bandages. "But I heal pretty quick."

"Yes. Me also," Thomas said, raising his shirt to reveal the scars again.

"Did a wolf do that?" Elias asked.

"No, a man," Thomas said, his eyes darkening. "I was very small, and I don't remember it well. It's better forgotten."

"A man did that?" Elias asked, touching the scars. "A white man?"

Thomas nodded, and Elias read bitterness in the Indian's deep brown eyes.

"Maybe when I learn to read and to write, I will understand white men better," Thomas said. "Sometimes I think they're all crazy."

44 |

"I know," Elias said, laughing. "Sometimes I think all Indians are crazy. But I'm learning, too."

"You fought the wolf."

"You did. I went along."

"No, you could have gone back. You stayed. I saw your eyes. The warrior spirit was there."

"What's that?"

"The part of you that says you will guard your house. It's what makes you unafraid."

"But I *was* afraid," Elias explained.

Thomas shook his head and searched out an explanation. No words seemed to come, though, and Elias frowned.

"Maybe white men aren't the same," Thomas finally said. "I don't know. It's difficult to know what another feels."

"Yes," Elias agreed.

"But trust my words. The spirit was there. You killed the wolves, two of them. Now the spirit of the wolf, his courage and cunning, belong to you."

"To me?"

"He marked you," Thomas said, pointing to Elias's bandaged leg. "And he left his tooth."

Elias started to ask about the tooth, but before the words could leave his lips, Thomas produced a long strip of leather. At one end was a large white tooth. Thomas placed the tooth on Elias's chest, then tied the two loose ends behind the injured boy's neck.

"It's a necklace," Elias said, smiling as he touched the tooth.

"More than that," Thomas said, confusion again flooding his face as he fought to find an explanation. "It is the tooth that marked you, the wolf's tooth. Inside the tooth is the wolf's spirit."

"I don't understand."

"The power, the courage. It will make you strong. It will protect you."

"Like a charm," Elias said, grinning.

"A ch-arm?" Thomas asked.

"That's what a white man would call it," Elias explained. "Charm. It means something that brings you good fortune."

"Yes," Thomas said, smiling.

Elias then listened as Thomas told of that first day of school, of the young Caddos who'd come, and of the slates Elias's father had presented to each student. Before the tale was completed, Elias's mother appeared, and Mr. Walsh followed shortly. Thomas left to fetch water for the horses, and Elias lay back and rested.

His mother made soup for dinner, but Elias had little appetite. His stomach was disturbed, and that troubled his mother as much as the tear in his thigh.

"I wouldn't worry about it, Mama," Mr. Walsh said as Elias finished. "He'll be his old self soon enough. Truth is, it's not a bad way to avoid a little work."

Elias would have grown angry had he not seen the sparkle in his father's eyes. And later that night it was Peter Walsh who carried Elias to a makeshift bed near the fireplace.

"You didn't expect your mother to give up her bed two nights, did you?" Elias's father asked.

"No, sir," Elias said, knowing the wound wasn't too

serious if his father felt it safe to move him. His father's arms seemed stronger than he remembered, and though his thigh ached, the pain wasn't sharp like before.

"Did Thomas bring you this?" Mr. Walsh asked, touching the wolf's tooth.

"It's from the wolf that bit me. The tooth came out. I suppose it was when I hit the wolf with a rock. Thomas says it will protect me from harm."

"Well, I think that's my job, son."

"Not anymore," Elias told him. "Out here on the frontier, boys grow up faster. Besides, you're going to be awful busy. I can look after myself."

"Think you can?"

"If you don't mind patching me up now and then," Elias said, laughing.

"Your mama'll have both our hides if you do something like this again anytime soon, son."

"I'll try to stay clear of wolves."

His father knelt beside him for a few minutes, and Elias knew the man was saying a prayer. Then Mr. Walsh touched Elias's chest and crossed the room to the other bed.

Elias remained in the cabin the rest of the week, letting the jagged tear in his leg heal. His mother changed the dressing twice, and on Saturday, she bathed the leg and pronounced it mending. The flesh was knitting itself together, and the less serious gashes on his shin were scabbed over. Thomas made a crutch from a live oak limb, and by Sunday, Elias was hopping around.

"Time you started earning your keep," his father told

Elias Monday morning. When the Indians arrived for school, Elias found himself assigned the task of helping the second class with their lessons.

Elias recognized most of his students. There were the Jackson boys, Sam and Joseph, together with Austin Crowheart and Andy Riversnake. After their meeting at the Brazos, Elias wasn't sure he entirely trusted any of them, though Sam and Austin, the eldest at twelve, were both shorter than Elias. All of them appeared oddly shy.

At least they won't be calling me White Bottom, Elias thought as he led them to their bench.

The other boy in the class, an Anadarko boy of eleven called Jack Larkin, gazed longingly at two other Anadarko children in the third class, both left to the care of Alice Rogers.

Alice's group was the largest. The two younger Anadarko boys had been grouped with three Caddo girls and the Jacksons' seven-year-old brother Bob. Elias's father had kept for himself the older children, all boys of fourteen. Thomas moved about the little one-room schoolhouse, translating instructions to the pupils.

Elias was prepared for those first weeks to be difficult, but he hadn't imagined anything like what actually occurred. The better part of the day was spent naming objects, then repeating them over and over again until the children could call them by their English names.

Afterward, they'd stand in turn and recite the letters of the alphabet. Before long Elias himself wasn't sure if *d* followed *c* or if *a* didn't really sound like *off*.

But lessons were only part of the problem. Some mornings the boys arrived at the schoolhouse nearly naked. The girls often wrapped themselves in blankets, and the little ones wore flour sacks with a hole cut in the top. None of them bothered with underthings, and when recess was called, most shed whatever they wore and ran to the river.

"My, my," Mrs. Walsh would remark, shaking her head as one of the Caddos raced past her washing. "This will never do."

So among Elias's more difficult chores was the task of measuring each of the boys for a pair of trousers. Alice tended to the girls, and Thomas was responsible for explaining why the crazy whites wanted to wrap lengths of twine around waists and shoulders to measure them.

Mrs. Walsh spent almost every waking moment afterward cutting and sewing clothes. The bolts of fabric grew smaller and smaller as each child acquired civilized clothing. Thomas insisted clothes be changed each day, and a careful watch was kept to see that it was done. Actually, that was easy since Mrs. Walsh had only two designs for shirts and dresses, a flowery poplin and a light blue solid, to be worn on alternate days. Trousers were made of the heavier denim. Underclothes were made from scraps or from what curtain material Alice had left.

"At last I feel like we've accomplished something," Mrs. Walsh declared when the entire school lined up appropriately clad.

Thomas and Elias exchanged knowing smiles and kept their thoughts to themselves. They'd discovered the Jackson boys rode the two miles to the school bare as ever, then put on shirts and trousers in the nearby trees.

But in truth, the Indian children were getting used to the clothes better than they were adjusting to their new language. The vowels were hard to say, and the words often remained foreign. The younger ones did better. The oldest of the boys appeared less and less often, especially as autumn approached and their hands were required in the fields.

Young Bob Jackson made some progress with his numbers, and Thomas was amazing. Of the others, most tried, but some seemed ready to surrender. Jack Larkin would sit beside Elias and whisper words Elias couldn't understand. Sometimes the boy would touch the wolf's tooth and smile. But a - b - c was the limit of his writing progress.

Once outside, the children really came to life. They excelled at every game Mr. Walsh presented. They ran with the wind, wrestled like veteran warriors, and rode like they were born on horseback.

"They know what has always been important," Thomas explained one morning when none of the children appeared. "The sky is full of thunder. A storm comes."

Sure enough, the earth soon shook with the fury of a cloudburst, and oceans of rain fell.

"It's hard becoming a white man," Thomas went on to say. "You must make the right mark on your slate and remember which letters make which words. Indians need only their hearts and the land. The food is there to eat, the water to drink."

"You don't have to become a white man," Elias said. "School won't do that to you."

"It's happening already," Thomas said, pointing to the moccasins on his feet and the shirt on his back. "Sometimes I think I should ride away to where the buffalo run.

But the Comanches are there, and they would kill me. No, my father's path is the only one I can take. And to walk it, I need to read and write."

Once Elias discarded his crutch and returned to the barn, Thomas's education accelerated. Thomas was never content to perform the lessons Mr. Walsh gave the school-children. Thomas carried the blueback speller and the McGuffey reader into the barn and slaved away at them. Often Elias would help, reading new words and reviewing old ones.

"Will you become a teacher like your father?" Thomas asked one night as they worked with numbers.

"I don't know," Elias said, checking Thomas's addition. "I once wanted to be a doctor, but I'm not sure anymore. Seeing blood makes me sick. I might become a lawyer. My brother's working at it right now."

"What does a lawyer do? Make laws?"

"Not exactly, although some become senators and such. Then they do make the laws. Most lawyers just work to make sure people get what they're entitled to. They study the law and make sure it's followed. They protect people from getting cheated by other people."

Elias looked into Thomas's eyes and smiled. Thomas understood very little of what Elias had said. It was no wonder. Laws were complicated. Josh said it took years of hard studying to know what they were all about. And here Thomas was working at simple math.

The learning wasn't all one-sided, though. Elias began acquiring a working knowledge of the Tonkawa language. He also learned how to make snares and skin the small animals he and Thomas trapped. Stories were swapped, and gradually Elias began to suspect what it had once been like to belong to the Tonkawa tribe.

"All that is long past, though," Thomas often remarked. "It won't be like that for me."

6.

September arrived, and with the completion of harvest, new students appeared at the school. Few older than Thomas stayed long, though, and none of the newcomers were girls.

"Even the white people out here aren't much for educating their daughters," Mr. Walsh grumbled. "Only girls like Alice Rogers, whose fathers are army officers, doctors, or judges, get much of a chance to learn to read. It's a shame."

Elias's mother just shrugged her shoulders and mumbled, "It's a man's world." Elias grinned. It might be a man's world, but he knew who did most of the deciding in *his* family. It wasn't his father.

September saw the beginnings of real progress for the Indian students at the agency school. Most could speak spotty English now, even little Jack Larkin, and several could recite the alphabet. Austin Crowheart and Thomas were stumbling through McGuffey, and Alice had her little ones counting through twenty.

Cooler weather made trousers less objectionable, and even the Jacksons had grown accustomed to riding in their britches. Mrs. Walsh had already started on the first jackets, though she'd abandoned the notion of introducing neckties after Thomas hinted there might be open rebellion.

Autumn brought the first of a long line of visitors to the little school. The first to come were army officers. Later some state officials arrived with Major Neighbors. A minister and his wife followed. Soon teachers, politicians, even a pair of bankers streamed by. The curious and the skeptical, Mr. Walsh called them, each eager to see for himself that the tax dollar was getting its worth.

"You can't blame them, really," Captain Rogers remarked. "We haven't been very successful with the Comanches. Most are still out on the range, and the cattle and horse raids continue. On top of that, the corn crop has largely failed."

"What did you expect?" Elias asked. "The land's poor, and not much corn was planted."

"I know," the captain said. "But if the tribes can't make themselves self-sufficient, I'm afraid they'll suffer even more. Too many people in the government want all the Indians out of Texas, even the Caddos."

As the weather turned cooler, Elias began to notice many of the children were growing thin. Back in the summer, the Walshes had issued flour weekly to families whose children attended school, but only a few had drawn their ration every week. Now the line had grown long, and even though Captain Rogers often brought barrels of beef or other goods down from Fort Belknap, there was never as much as was needed.

"I've tried to explain it to the governor," the captain said, sighing. "Some of the corn crop wasn't dried properly. The Caddos aren't used to grinding flour, or storing it, either."

Elias had heard all the reasons a hundred times. They hadn't mattered in the summer when the river ran swiftly and fish were easily had. Game was plentiful, especially birds. As a chill came to the air, it seemed the countryside was as bare as the storehouse.

"They never complain," Elias told Thomas. "I know Austin hasn't had anything to eat at lunchtime in a week. Jack's ribs stick out halfway through his skin. He can barely keep his trousers on."

"They're young, but they've learned," Thomas said sadly. "It does no good to complain. I remember once when I lived with Raven. All the children were hungry. The babies began to die. Food was supposed to arrive, but always it was late. A wagon would break down, or a storehouse would burn. So we were told."

"What did your uncle do?" Elias asked. "He couldn't just let everyone starve."

"We weren't far from the buffalo range. Winter isn't the time to ride to the hunt, but the hunger in our bellies gave wings to our horses. We hunted. Soon the cries of the children were quiet, and we were strong again."

"Are there any buffalo around here?" Elias asked. "Maybe we could shoot some and take the meat to the Caddos and Anadarkos."

"The buffalo valleys are too far, and we are too young to go alone. Comanches would find us."

"Isn't there anything we can do?"

"I will think about it."

"So will I."

Elias did more than think, though. He spoke with Captain Rogers.

"If we could gather up all the men and hunt buffalo," Elias said, "we could get enough meat to last through winter. Thomas says that's how the Indians have always survived."

"The Caddos have been farmers a long time, Elias. The Kiowas and Comanches are the hunters. They still are. I'm afraid the Comanches aren't going to let a small band of Caddos take to the buffalo range even if the whole Second Cavalry rode with them."

"So what do we do, just let them starve?"

Captain Rogers smiled and placed a heavy hand on Elias's shoulder. "I see they've won you to their side, too. I've written a dozen letters, Elias. There are cattle wandering the range. My men pick up a few maverick cows when they can. That's why there's been some meat."

"Maybe Thomas and I could . . ."

"Haven't you had enough adventure?" the captain asked, pointing toward Elias's leg. "But maybe . . ."

"Maybe what?"

"It's been a long time since we've had a holiday, hasn't

it? Perhaps we ought to declare a hunting holiday. Deer are plentiful to the north."

"The hides would be good for clothes, too," Elias said, remembering one of Thomas's stories.

"I'll speak to your father about it," the captain promised. "You don't suppose you and Thomas might like to go with me, do you?"

"Papa may have something to say about that," Elias said, sighing. "I would like to go, though."

"I'll ask your father and mother. No shotguns this time. I'll loan you a carbine."

"Yes, sir!" Elias said, trotting off to tell Thomas.

It was another week before the longed-for holiday arrived, and eager anticipation made those seven days the longest Elias could recall. Twice Captain Rogers took Elias and Thomas out to practice firing the carbines, and that only made the delay that much harder. When they finally rode north, Elias could hardly control his enthusiasm.

"Remember," Captain Rogers warned. "We're not riding after buffalo. Deer have good ears. All your jabbering will scare a buck halfway to Pennsylvania."

Elias nodded and bit his lip. But it was hard to ride quietly to an adventure.

All day they rode through the thickets above the river in search of deer tracks, but the soft sand revealed nothing.

"The Caddos have been here," Thomas said, pointing to a moccasin track. "They've hunted the deer here since summer. He's not stupid, the deer. He runs to high ground."

By twilight they'd found nothing. Captain Rogers led the

way to a clearing beside a small creek. There the three would-be hunters made camp.

"Not much of a supper," Elias grumbled as they chewed cold biscuits beside a small fire. "We should be eating venison steaks."

Thomas offered Elias another biscuit, but Elias shook his head.

"It's not me I'm really worried about," Elias explained. "I wanted to take something back for Austin and little Jack."

"Yes," Thomas said, clasping Elias's hand. "We will make a prayer."

Elias bowed his head, but Thomas walked to the edge of the creek, unbuttoned his shirt, and chanted to the stars. Elias stared in disbelief, but Captain Rogers motioned for silence.

"He's praying to the spirit of the deer," the captain explained. "It's his way. You go on and pray your way."

"But . . ."

"It's best," the captain said, bowing his own head and motioning for Elias to do likewise.

Elias searched for words as Thomas screamed out Tonkawa phrases and danced around. Lastly a song drifted across the camp, and Elias hummed along.

"We will find a deer in the morning," Thomas assured them when he returned. "But we must not take any of the meat for ourselves."

"Sure," Elias agreed.

"If that's how you want it," Captain Rogers said.

They then crowded around the campfire, and Thomas related the tale of his father's first clash with Comanches down on the Colorado River. The story was full of action and excitement, and Elias was sorry to have it end.

"You now," Thomas said, nudging Elias in the ribs.

For Elias's part, he told of a trip he'd taken aboard a sloop bound for New Orleans. But Thomas asked question after question, and after a while, Elias noticed his friend lost interest.

"It's too far away, Elias," Captain Rogers told him afterward. "He can't imagine anything like an ocean, or a ship with sails. To most Indians, there's just the here and now."

"But he told me he came to the school to learn reading and writing. To prepare for his future."

"Those are his father's words. Joseph has lived with the whites a long time. He thinks like we do. Still, most of the Indian boys don't do awfully well at the school. It's hard for them to understand that the world will change so much. It's too different."

Elias nodded. He knew what it was like to journey into a different world. Life at the agency was so different from Waco. But he was too tired to worry more that night. He fell into a sound sleep.

Thomas stirred them a little before dawn.

"Come," he whispered. "I've seen the deer."

Elias pulled on his trousers and loaded his carbine. Thomas led the way. Elias and Captain Rogers followed. A hundred yards upstream Thomas located a pair of large bucks surrounded by three or four does. Each hunter marked his target, and the carbines fired together. Elias watched as the doe he'd picked fell to one leg, then collapsed. Thomas had killed the buck on the left, and Captain Rogers shot another doe.

The rest of the animals scattered like leaves before the wind, and Thomas chanted again to the sky.

"Three deer will fill many bellies," he told Elias. "Now we must begin the skinning and dress the meat."

By midafternoon the animals had been skinned, and the meat was packed on the backs of the horses. The hunters then started toward Indian Springs. By nightfall meat had been delivered to each of the scattered cabins along the Brazos.

Elias's mother and father were only mildly angry that the boys had stretched their holiday into a second day. Few of the children had appeared at school anyway.

"They'll be back tomorrow," Elias told his father. "They just had to go farther to find game than they figured."

"I'm just glad you're home," Mrs. Walsh said, hugging Elias for the first time in weeks.

"You shouldn't worry," Elias said, lifting the wolf's tooth from beneath his shirt. "I'm safe."

After a wonderful hot dinner, Elias and Thomas retired to the barn to work on the hides.

"You've brought us much honor," Thomas said as they tacked the skins on the wall.

"I did?" Elias asked. "It was your prayer."

"But your idea," Thomas reminded him. "I don't always understand your ways, Elias. Sometimes you're crazy. Wearing coats to supper in summer! But in your heart, you are a Tonkawa."

Elias warmed as Thomas gripped his hand.

"I'm glad you're my friend, too," Elias said. "What will we do with the hides?"

"We'll make your mother a dress," Thomas said, laughing at the thought.

"Sure," Elias agreed. "Seems only fair after she's sewn for half the valley."

With that decided, they climbed into their blankets and let exhaustion sweep them away into a peaceful sleep.

7.

There were few other opportunities for Elias to escape the confines of the agency school in the days that followed. More and more visitors appeared, and often Elias and Alice found themselves tending to the needs of the students while his father was preoccupied with showing guests around. Sometimes Elias resented the extra responsibility, and he'd grumble about the hours devoted to listening to Sam Jackson repeating the alphabet.

"I know you'd rather have your nose in that French history, Lias, but your papa is more than just a teacher here," Elias's mother told him. "He's responsible for the welfare of the people. Why do you think we received the extra flour last week? Where do you think those crates of chickens came from?"

"I thought . . ." Elias started to say.

"Your papa convinced Senator Holland to increase supplies. The chickens were a gift from the Quaker missions."

Elias observed the visitors more closely afterward, and he often encouraged his charges to perform for their audience. The Jackson boys especially enjoyed the attention. Only little Jack Larkin shied away from the strangers.

"You can't trust white men," Jack told Elias later in surprisingly good English.

"But I'm a white man," Elias explained, pressing Jack's small hand against his own. "See. My hair's blond. My eyes are blue. You can't be any whiter than that!"

"Ah, but you wear the wolf's tooth," Jack said, touching the necklace hidden under Elias's shirt.

"And my father?"

"In the beginning, I wasn't sure. He *is* a good man, but he doesn't know the whites like we do."

"We?"

Jack tapped Elias's chest, then pointed to the Caddo boys on the nearby bench.

"You mean the Indians?" Elias asked.

Jack said nothing. Caution was written in his eyes.

The final visitors of October included half a company of soldiers, led by Captain Rogers himself. They didn't come to examine the schoolhouse, though.

"Word has come that Comanches were sighted upriver," the captain explained. "We're here to patrol. I've arranged for part of the detachment to stay with you just in case."

"Do you think that's necessary?" Mr. Walsh asked. "Won't that alarm the others?"

"Alice is here," Captain Rogers said. "Your boy, too. Besides, I've got a man with me who's getting to be a regular nuisance. He's been pleading with the major for a week's leave, and I suppose you'd say this is the ideal moment.''

Captain Rogers motioned toward the soldiers, and one man rode forward. Elias noticed long black hair flowed out of a regular cavalryman's hat. The twin stripes of a corporal appeared on one sleeve of a uniform tunic, but the man wore buckskin trousers and moccasins.

"Peter, Abigail, Elias, I'd like to introduce Joseph Three Feathers," the captain said, nodding to the scout. "Is Thomas about?"

Joseph's weary eyes seemed to brighten at the mention of his son, and Elias stepped away from his parents.

"He's with the horses," Elias explained. "I can take you there."

"Thank you," Joseph said, stepping down from the saddle and leaving his horse to the attention of one of the soldiers.

"He's my friend," Elias whispered as they walked.

"It's good he has a friend," the scout said, slowing to match Elias's pace. "It is a difficult time for him."

"For me, too. We help each other."

Joseph nodded.

Elias took Thomas's father inside the barn. They found Thomas rubbing liniment into the shoulder of one of the mules. Thomas gazed with surprise at his father but restrained any urge to greet the man.

"I guess you two will be wanting to talk some," Elias said, backing out of the barn. "I imagine Papa's got chores for me to do."

Joseph Three Feathers nodded, but Thomas said nothing. Father and son seemed frozen a dozen feet from each other, and Elias didn't understand. He expected Thomas to race to his father's side, but instead the young Tonkawa continued his work.

Elias went back outside, sadly shaking his head. And he says *I'm* crazy, Elias thought. He hasn't seen his father in months, and now he practically ignores the man.

Elias was just as confused when Thomas appeared as always for supper. His father ate with the other soldiers in spite of Mrs. Walsh's invitation to join the family. Afterward, though, Elias spotted Thomas with Joseph beside the river. There, away from everyone, Thomas leaned against his father, and the two jabbered away like a pair of magpies.

In that next week, Elias seldom saw his friend. Except for the hours they shared sleeping in the barn and the time at the school, Thomas would totally vanish. Elias knew his friend was off walking or riding with the father who'd be leaving all too soon. And when the day finally came that Captain Rogers and the other soldiers returned, Thomas bid his father farewell as quietly as he'd said hello.

"I guess since they didn't find any Comanches, they won't keep your father at the fort," Elias said as they lay in their blankets that night.

"No," Thomas whispered.

Elias thought he detected a tremor in Thomas's speech, but it was too dark to detect anything more.

"It must be hard to be away from your family," Elias said, sitting up.

"I've grown used to it," Thomas answered.

"How do you grow used to being lonely?" Elias asked. "I don't see how . . ."

"Sometimes my path is a difficult one," Thomas said, stirring slightly. "My father once told me the harder a man's path, the stronger he becomes."

If he survives, Elias thought, closing his eyes and laying back in his bed.

The next day, after school was dismissed, Elias followed Thomas into the barn. As they saw to the needs of the stock, Thomas pointed to the three skins on the wall.

"It's time we worked those hides," Thomas said, running his fingers along the nose of his horse.

"I'll borrow one of Mama's dresses. We can use it for a pattern."

"You don't wish to use the twine again?" Thomas asked, reminding Elias of the strand of twine they'd used to measure the Indian children at the schoolhouse. Elias burst out laughing at the notion of wrapping twine around his mother's waist.

"It'd spoil the surprise, too," Elias pointed out.

So it was settled. As soon as afternoon chores were finished, Elias stole over to the house and snatched his mother's gray dress. By the time he returned, Thomas had the hides stretched out on the small table more often used for repairing harness.

Thomas took the dress and stared at it in confusion.

"I suppose it's easier to make a shirt," Elias said, noticing the many folds his mother had made in the skirt. "But we'll manage."

"Easier than hunting a wolf."

"Much," Elias agreed.

Though Thomas lacked experience making women's clothes, from buckskin or not, and Elias's sole tailoring talents amounted to patching a tear in his trousers, they soon began shaping a skirt from one of the hides. The upper part of the dress was much more of a challenge, but Thomas had a sharp eye, and he managed to cut pieces of doeskin to match the parts of Mrs. Walsh's dress. The sewing would be another matter.

"I suppose you've had to learn to do for yourself," Elias said as Thomas produced a spiral of sinewy thread. "I've always had somebody around to do things like make my clothes."

Thomas winced as he pricked his finger with the needle.

"When I was eight, Mama tried to teach me to sew," Elias said, sighing. "I'm afraid to say I was a failure."

"Tonkawa boys learn to make moccasins. Later, they take the hide of the deer or the coat of the buffalo and make clothing. When my brothers were born, my father even then scouted for the soldiers. Raven, my mother's brother, helped me make shoes for the little ones. Later, I made coats to keep off the winter chill."

"You taught them to swim, too," Elias said, remembering that first time he and Thomas had gone to the river. "Tell me about your brothers."

"I don't have brothers," Thomas said, setting aside the sewing a moment as a deep sadness flooded his face.

"But you did once."

"Long ago."

"What happened?"

"A white woman came to our village," Thomas said,

swallowing the sadness and continuing with the sewing as he spoke. "She said she would teach us the white man's words, the white man's ways. Her husband was a farmer, and he showed us the plow. But her little ones grew ill with the spotted sickness."

Thomas paused and pricked the flesh of his arm so that tiny red spots of blood appeared.

"Smallpox?" Elias asked, shifting his feet.

"No," Thomas said, shaking his head. "I have heard of the pox. It was the spotted sickness."

"Measles," Elias mumbled, remembering how he'd raged with fever after contracting the disease from Joshua.

"Soon all the little ones were sick. The medicine chiefs prayed. We danced and fasted. One by one the little ones caught fire and died. My brothers were near the first."

"You didn't catch it yourself?"

"Yes, but I was older," Thomas explained. "Raven took me to the sweat lodge. My fever was cast away, and I grew stronger."

"I had it, too. When I was five or so. I close to died."

"It was after the illness that I lived at the fort," Thomas said, setting aside the needle long enough to wipe his forehead.

"It must have been hard for your mother to let you leave."

"The spotted sickness took her, too," Thomas muttered. "And Raven. Of all my family only my father remained."

Elias extended a hand toward his friend, but Thomas stepped away.

"I've told no one of this," Thomas said, his eyes growing red. "You must hold it in your heart, telling not even your mother and father. Among our people, death is common. It comes with the winter snow and the summer rain."

"That doesn't make it any easier," Elias said. "It still hurts."

"Yes, but the path of the Tonkawa has always been hard. I must walk it alone to be strong."

"Nobody's ever stronger for being by himself, Thomas. I remember one summer my folks left me with Aunt Ellen in Galveston. I was so alone I thought I'd choke. I wouldn't tell anybody, not my aunt or uncle or my cousins. I just sat alone at night and hoped to die. If I'd let them know, they might've helped."

"How does a man grow to be strong if another does his work, Elias? If your father read you the words in your book, would you have learned to read?"

"That's not what I mean at all," Elias complained. "I know you have to learn to do things. But you shouldn't be afraid to have friends."

Thomas smiled, and Elias took the needle and tried his hand at sewing. He couldn't drive the needle through the thick hide, though, and Thomas resumed the work.

"Once I asked my father why the Tonkawa didn't fight the whites as the Comanches do," Thomas said, moving the needle through the fabric with sudden ease. "He said we were a small tribe and that perhaps we were too gentle a people. The Comanches kill all in their path. They ask no mercy from their enemies, and they offer none. They still ride the buffalo valleys, while the Tonkawas and the Caddos build lodges of wood and hope their corn will grow."

"They can't stay out there forever," Elias said, sadly shaking his head. "Then who'll be the smarter? You will know how to read and write. You'll be able to make a good life for yourselves. The Comanches, those who don't get killed fighting soldiers, will just be starting."

"Maybe."

"But you'd still trade places with them, wouldn't you?" Elias asked. "So you could hunt the buffalo and ride the prairies."

Thomas nodded, and Elias smiled.

"Maybe I would, too," Elias admitted. "But you said it yourself. We have to walk our own paths."

"Yes," Thomas said solemnly.

It took a half dozen afternoons all totaled before the dress was completed. Even then it would never have been mistaken for something out of Mrs. Brewster's storefront window back in Waco. But when Elias and Thomas presented the dress to Mrs. Walsh, the woman drew back in amazement.

"For me?" she gasped. "I don't understand. I've had no birthday."

"Because you make clothes for all the little ones," Thomas explained.

"I'm not sure this isn't Thomas's way of getting back at you for insisting on neckties every Sunday," Mr. Walsh said, grinning as he held up the slightly lopsided garment.

"Nonsense," the woman said, pulling the boys to her side and planting a kiss on each of their foreheads. "I'll treasure this."

"Maybe you should," Elias said as he and an embarrassed Thomas retreated. "Considering the number of times we pricked our fingers, we're not likely to be in a real hurry to make another."

They all shared a brief moment of laughter before Mrs. Walsh set the dress aside and waved toward the dinner table.

"It was a good idea," Elias whispered to his friend.

"Yes," Thomas agreed.

And as they sat down at the table, Elias hoped Thomas felt a part of the family. Solitude, for all the strength it might bring, was a heavy burden to carry into winter.

8.

Of all the seasons, Elias liked winter the least. It was a time of death, of despair. It was in December that both his grandfathers had died. A January chill had carried off his little cousin Jeremiah. Even in Waco, in the house with its tall stone fireplace, a chill crept through the night, bringing fevers or coughing fits. Old people complained of weary bones, and the children shivered on their way to school.

Winter along the Brazos proved to be a hostile time. Howling winds roared down from the north, their icy fingers cutting through even the warmest clothes until they tore into a man's insides. Great seas of snow drifted across the rocky ground toward the middle of December, and even after they melted away, their touch could be felt on frigid windows and floors.

Often Elias found himself fighting off the numbing cold

from his toes and fingers, especially while carrying wood or fetching water. Even on the brightest days, a heavy fog greeted his waking eyes. Sunrise would be late, and slivers of ice dangling from the eaves of the barn or the branches of trees would give the place a glittering, silvery appearance.

The onset of winter brought problems. The gravest one was that the flow of supplies to Fort Belknap and from there to the agency slowed and occasionally stopped altogether. It seemed unfair to Elias that now, when the Indians needed their rations more than ever, they should have to settle for less. Game was scarce, and even weekend hunting forays with Captain Rogers turned up little in the way of fresh meat. The children's faces grew even thinner, and Elias bit his lip and swallowed the bitterness that was spreading through the whole agency.

"I feel like I've betrayed them," Elias's father said one evening at dinner. "I promised that if the children attended my classes, there'd be provisions of flour, spices, even meat from time to time. Now look at us! We barely have enough to feed ourselves, and the supply wagons are two weeks overdue."

"It wasn't your promise, Peter," Mrs. Walsh objected. "You weren't the one who broke it, either. It's Major Neighbors' responsibility. He's a good man. He'll find a way to get us the supplies we need."

But as the days crept on toward Christmas, Elias noticed his father's despair grow heavier. Many of the students at the school arrived shivering, walking on feet clothed with strips of torn blankets. Moccasins had worn too thin to be of use. Even the Jackson boys took to walking, not, as Elias had suspected, because the trails had grown too treacherous, but because the animals had been eaten.

"It's a sad time for them," Thomas said as he and Elias exercised the mules. "Even the dogs have been eaten. I'm afraid some of the people will die soon if food doesn't come."

Captain Rogers made the same observation to Elias later that week.

"Winter's always been a trial on the plains, but this is terrible. I can't stay here and watch a people wither and die."

The captain left the next day, returning toward nightfall with a wagon loaded with flour and beans.

"The soldiers agreed to share their rations," the captain explained. "We've bought a precious few days. But if we're not resupplied soon, I hate to think what will happen."

Mrs. Walsh took it upon herself to carry a basket of biscuits to the schoolhouse each morning, even though the flour keg in the pantry was growing alarmingly close to empty. Alice boiled tea on the old Franklin stove beside the door, and when a rabbit or a possum was snared by one of Thomas's traps, the whole school enjoyed a rare soup spiced by native herbs. Only three chickens remained in the coop, a white rooster and a pair of brown hens. Their eggs, often as not, were boiled and sent home with the thinnest of the children.

A week before Christmas, Elias was aroused from a deathlike slumber by a piercing cry. It was followed by another, and another after that.

"Wolves," he mumbled, shaking himself awake. "They've come back."

"Yes," Thomas agreed, sitting up. "It's the season of wolves. They come to prey on the dead."

"We're not dead yet," Elias declared, pulling on his clothes and wrapping a blanket around his shoulders. "Papa still leaves the shotgun here for us."

"Not tonight," Thomas said, reaching out and holding Elias in place. "I hear two, maybe three of them. You are weary, and we don't know where they are."

"I'm still wearing the wolf's tooth," Elias reminded his friend. "I'll come to no harm."

"Even a wolf's tooth doesn't guard against foolishness. We will scout the hillside when morning comes. We'll find these wolves."

Elias read confidence in Thomas's eyes and reluctantly returned to bed. But the howling of the wolves permitted scant rest. The sun found both boys exhausted, their eyes streaked with crimson clouds.

"I heard wolves last night, Papa," Elias told his father. "Thomas and I are going to look for tracks this morning."

"You'll do no such thing," Mr. Walsh declared. "You were fortunate to escape your last encounter with wolves. Besides, I need you at the schoolhouse."

"No, you don't," Elias said, gazing intently into his father's eyes. "There aren't but five or six attending anymore, and they speak some English. You can manage."

"Let them have the chickens," Elias's mother said from the doorway. "What difference does it make? There won't be anyone left if the supply wagon isn't here soon."

"Maybe we'll spot a deer while we're out," Elias said, forcing a smile onto his face.

"No deer was ever so swift that it could escape the

hungry eyes of a hundred Indians," Mr. Walsh said, sadly watching as Thomas appeared and handed Elias the shotgun.

"You see how it's got to be, don't you, Papa?" Elias pleaded. "We have to go."

"I could order you to stay, son," Peter Walsh said, resting a firm hand on Elias's shoulder.

"Don't," Elias whispered, slipping away from his father's hand, then touching the man's dangling hand. "I know you'd go yourself, but you've got the school to worry about."

"Alice could . . ."

"Papa, we'll be all right," Elias said, shifting his eyes to his mother a second, then returning to his father. "Thomas knows these hills. We won't take any chances."

"See you don't!" Mrs. Walsh called out then. "Don't stay gone so long we'll fret."

"Home for supper," Elias promised.

With that decided, he followed Thomas down the frost-covered trail, pulling two cartridges from his pocket and holding them ready for use in case of trouble. But as they wove their way through the junipers of the hillsides, they saw nothing more than the paw print of a skunk or raccoon.

"I guess it'd be easier to tell where they are at night," Elias commented as they searched the sandy ground for some hint of their quarry. "At least we'd hear them."

"Night is the sister of the wolf," Thomas said. "He can hide in the dark and wait for us to come."

"The wolves wouldn't know we're coming."

"They know," Thomas said, heading to the east. "They remember."

"They do?"

"Have you forgotten you carry the wolf's tooth?" Thomas asked. "He left his mark on your leg."

"It might not be the same wolf," Elias said, laughing nervously. "The whole country's full of animals. You can't know it was one of the wolves howling last night."

"I know," Thomas declared, turning around so that Elias could read a mixture of dread and confidence in the Tonkawa's eyes. "I feel him already, and we are far away."

Elias felt a strange sensation creeping up his spine, and he froze.

"You feel it, too," Thomas said, waving for his friend to lead the way. "Let your heart guide us, Elias. Use the strength and courage the wolf gave you."

Elias touched the tooth dangling around his neck. His chest seemed to warm in spite of a shrill wind whistling through the trees. And as he made his way through the forest of wicked briars and fragile arms of pencil cactus, he kept a sharp eye out for any glimpse of a long gray shape.

"Do you remember now?" Thomas asked as they stepped into a clearing facing a great pile of boulders.

Elias nodded. The air filled with an eerie silence. He could smell something terribly foul in the air as he loaded the shotgun.

"Yes," Thomas whispered as they searched the rocks. "The smell of death."

Theirs or ours? Elias wondered. But before the thought was even complete, he heard the low growl of the wolves. Shortly, two dark green eyes stared out from behind the long pointed snout of a gray wolf. Rows of jagged white teeth flashed in the sunlight, and Elias shuddered.

"Is he the one?" Thomas asked.

"I don't know," Elias confessed. "I barely remember what happened."

"What do you feel?"

"No, that's not him," Elias said, suddenly turning to the left and lifting the shotgun to his shoulder. From out of the trees flew a fierce, dark-coated wolf, and Elias fired both barrels. The air filled with powder smoke, and for a moment, both boys were blinded. The blast tore the charging wolf apart, but even as Elias fought to reload the gun, the gray creature from the rocks stepped forth, uttering a low, challenging growl.

"Lord, help me," Elias prayed as he fumbled with the percussion caps. "Deliver me . . ."

Thomas pushed him back as the gray sprang into motion, snapping out with its furious teeth. Elias finally got the shotgun loaded, but by now Thomas was in the way, fending off the wolf with a juniper branch and jabbing out with a knife.

"Get out of the way!" Elias pleaded as the wolf pressed its attack. There was no hope of hitting the wolf and missing Thomas. Maybe with a rifle, but . . .

"Behind you!" Thomas screamed.

Elias turned just in time to be struck full force by an ivory-coated wolf of enormous power. The shotgun fired off harmlessly into the air, peppering the air with powder and momentarily stunning the attacking wolf.

"Use your knife," Thomas yelled. "Strike now."

But even as Elias set aside the shotgun and pulled his

knife, the white wolf stirred. Elias's blade plunged harmlessly into the ground where only an instant before the deadly creature had lain.

The wolves backed away, glaring at Thomas and Elias with fierce eyes that seemed to say, "Here we are! Strike us if you can, Two Wolves! I'll show you what it is to be a wolf, little white one. I'll teach you the feel of teeth sinking into your flesh. I'll bring your death!"

"Hold them off," Elias whispered. "I'll reload the gun."

Each time Elias made a move toward the shotgun, though, the two wolves started together toward Thomas.

It won't be easy this time, Elias thought as he edged closer to his friend. No shotgun to do the killing. No, this time it's knife against claw, me against him.

"Thomas?" Elias asked nervously.

"I know," Thomas said, bracing himself for the fight to come. "It's a challenge, my friend, and we must face it."

Elias swallowed the fear that was strangling him. It wouldn't have made sense a year ago, in Waco, where the greatest struggle had been with Latin chronicles or academy girls. He steadied his hands and picked up a branch to use as a club. As if they understood, too, that it was time to settle the issue, the wolves howled out a chilling cry. Then they raced forward.

It seemed to Elias that it took forever for the huge white wolf to cross the five yards that lay between them. All that time Elias prepared himself for the blow, considered his best course of action. In the end, Elias only managed to turn slightly, barely avoiding the collision. Still the razor-like claws of the creature tore away at his shirt and cut into his shoulder.

The force of the wolf sent Elias flying backward, but even so, he managed to strike out with the knife. The wolf howled in pain as the knife tore a gash from forefoot to hind leg across the belly.

"Elias?" Thomas called out as he struck down the gray wolf.

But there was no chance to respond. Instead Elias rolled twice, then lifted the knife as the staggering wolf lurched forward, its ivory flank flowing crimson red. Elias jabbed his club outward, and the wolf grasped it with its teeth. Claws struck out, but Elias escaped their force and struck out, in turn, with his knife.

"Elias!" Thomas screamed.

The wolf howled in pain as the knife struck swiftly, deep. But as the creature pulled away, the knife went, too. Elias felt his fingers lose their grip, and he lay on the earth, defenseless.

"Lord, help me," Elias prayed aloud while he struggled to crawl toward the shotgun. But as the wolf prepared a final lunge, Thomas raced by, splitting the air as he dove at the great white wolf, ripping away with knife blade in a fashion so savage that it gave the creature no hope of delivery. Elias stood frozen as Thomas drove his blade again and again into the heart of the wolf. Finally Thomas stepped back, and Elias gripped the blood-streaked hands of his friend.

"We were crazy to come out here," Elias said quietly as he touched the burning flesh of his shoulder.

"No," Thomas objected, shaking even now. "It was the land that made us come."

"How can that be?" Elias asked, wide-eyed.

"Raven told me long ago that before a man can walk the land, he must stand tall. He must feel the winter's chill and the burning face of summer. And he must test his spirit."

"How can he do that?"

"Look here," Thomas said, pointing to the three dead animals. "Long before my people or yours came to this place, the wolf was here. He hunted and killed all that fell within his shadow, but always he cried out in the night, 'Come, brave one. Come and face the claws and the teeth of the wolf! Come and find your death, and bring mine. Only the strong walk this place.'"

"I don't feel particularly strong," Elias said, wincing as he tore a strip of his shirt and pressed it against the three long, deep scratches that began at the collarbone and cut their way across his chest. "Truth is, I feel stupid. Captain Rogers would've come up here with a squad and shot those wolves up with carbines."

"He would never have found them," Thomas said, a strangely distant sparkle appearing in his eyes. "This was our test, my friend. The wolf spoke to us. Look."

Elias watched as Thomas turned the heavy head of the white wolf slightly. On the left side of the beast's jaw three teeth were missing.

"It *was* my wolf," Elias said, nodding.

"Yes," Thomas said. "Come, help me with the skinning."

"With what?" Elias cried out in disbelief. "The skinning? We're both bleeding. Let's go back and let Mama tend us."

"Have you forgotten the empty eyes of the children?" Thomas asked. "A hungry belly can be filled by the meat of a wolf as well as a deer. Warm coats can be made of wolf hides."

Elias shrugged his shoulders and followed his friend to the carcasses. Soon they were skinning the creatures, and by afternoon, they'd dragged the meat back to the house.

"Oh, my God!" Mrs. Walsh cried when she saw Elias's bloodied coat. "You've gotten yourself half-killed again!"

"No, Mama," Elias said, grinning to alleviate her fears. "It's not bad. The bleeding's stopped. We're going to ride out to the cabins and give the people this meat."

"You killed a deer?" Mrs. Walsh asked.

"No," Elias said nervously. "Three wolves."

Mrs. Walsh objected. "You can't eat—"

"You can eat anything if you're hungry enough," Thomas broke in.

9.

After helping Thomas load the bundles of meat onto one of the mules, Elias saddled a second animal while his friend readied the restless mustang pony.

"He smells the wolf," Thomas said, quieting his horse. "Horses and wolves—they aren't friends."

"No," Elias agreed, wondering if a wolf was welcomed as a visitor anywhere.

The two young riders spoke little more of wolves, though. Instead Thomas led the way down the dusty road toward the Caddo settlements.

All afternoon they appeared at cabins from Dry Creek to Indian Springs, presenting gifts of meat and sharing hope that the cold gray skies and the gnawing hunger of winter might soon pass. Where Elias had expected to meet grateful eyes and joyful shouts, he found instead a quiet nod from one of the women, a remembrance of an earlier hunting trip by some grandfather. No one spoke of thanks or tried to reward his benefactors.

"It's not our way," Thomas explained when Elias began grumbling. "When we have, we share. Understand, it's not us that's brought this food."

"It's not?" Elias cried in disbelief. "It's not my skin that's torn by wolf claws?"

Thomas grinned and shook his head.

"All that comes to us is sent by the spirits, Elias, my friend. The land gives. We only help."

But no matter how Thomas explained it, Elias would never really understand. It was like when he'd tried to tell Thomas about the voyage from New Orleans. There were simply too many differences between them.

It was approaching twilight when Thomas nudged his pony away from the Jacksons' cabin. The long ride teamed with the rigors of that morning and the chill winter air to send shivers of weariness through them.

"Only one bundle left," Elias noted, glancing at the back of the pack mule.

"For the Riversnakes," Thomas said, waving a thin finger into the distant haze.

Elias shook off the cold and smiled. He imagined little Andy appearing at the cabin door, those large brown eyes brightening as he sniffed out the meat. It had been days, maybe more than a week, since Andy had appeared at the agency. The ten-year-old half broke Elias's heart. As little Andy huddled beside the fire, his thin legs still trembled from the icy air outside. And when the boy finally removed his coat, Elias could see the sharp outline of ribs and shoulders through the thin fabric of Andy's shirt.

As Elias and Thomas approached the Riversnakes' cabin, Elias grew strangely nervous. There's no smoke from the chimney, he thought. Something's wrong!

Thomas shouted a Tonkawa greeting. But no sign of life appeared.

"Could be they've gone," Thomas said.

"Maybe they're too proud to take our gift," Elias suggested. "They might be ignoring us like at that cabin back at Dry Creek."

"Look," Thomas said, his face filling with alarm. "No smoke from a fire. Smell the air. Nothing!"

"Probably gone hunting."

Elias read his friend's eyes. The desire to believe was there, but it was overpowered by a terrifying chill that raced through the both of them. Thomas was first off his horse. By the time Elias dismounted, Thomas had burst through the door and on into the cabin.

"Well?" Elias called, running to the plank porch.

"Don't," Thomas said, retreating out the door and doing his best to block Elias from entering. "Don't . . . look!"

Elias stumbled as he watched terror invade Thomas's eyes. Never before had Thomas appeared really afraid, not even while stalking the wolves.

"I have to," Elias finally said, slipping under the Tonkawa's long arm and stepping quietly through the door. There, beside the hearth, sat the Riversnakes, Andy's small brother and sister squeezed between his parents. Andy himself lay beside his father, a small skeleton with flesh pasted upon bones. The little head rested on his father's proud shoulder.

"Don't," Thomas whispered as Elias stepped closer. All five figures were coated with an eerie white dust—frost. Elias rubbed the ice away from little Andy's sunken cheeks, touched the cold, stiff strands of raven hair. Nothing of the warmth, the brightness, of the child's smile remained. All had been stolen away in the night by that thief of winter, death.

"Ayy aah aah," Thomas bellowed, beginning a Tonkawa chant of some sort. On and on Thomas sang, pounding his feet harder and harder against the bare sandy floor as he danced.

Elias envied his friend. He wished he knew something to shout. Funerals among the Walshes had always been quiet, solemn occasions. Somehow it was more appropriate to shout and scream when you discovered a family starved and frozen in their own cabin!

"We never got you through all your numbers, Andy," Elias said as he continued to rub ice away from the boy's face. "I should have known you wouldn't stay home if you weren't in trouble. I should have ridden out here to see what was wrong. We should have hunted deer."

"Come," Thomas said, concluding his chant and leading Elias away. "It was their time."

"Their time?" Elias screamed. "Their time? They starved because we didn't have the flour to give them! Did you see the little ones? Their time? They weren't old enough to be dying!"

"Stop!" Thomas shouted, grabbing Elias's wrist and pulling him from the cabin. "What do you know? My brothers also were young! How old was my mother? You didn't send the cold winds from the north. You didn't drive off the deer or break the wagons' wheels. The spirits make life hard, not you or me. They say to a man, 'Be strong!' They send death to walk among the lodges."

"I don't believe in spirits walking around, freezing little kids to death."

"I've watched you pray. You believe. Oh, you call them something else. We have different words for house, for book, even for horse and man. From the time the sun was placed in the sky, people have died. Some old, some young. It's not changed. Sometimes death comes, taking away even the small. Sometimes they welcome it."

"I'll never believe that," Elias said, shaking his head.

"It freed them from their pain," Thomas said, forcing Elias into a sitting position at the edge of the porch. "Now I must—"

"Must what?" Elias asked as Thomas turned back toward the door.

"The ground's too hard to dig graves," Thomas said, suddenly wild-eyed. "It's like at Fort Mason. The soldiers would not like us to raise them above the ground. It's best we give them to the fire."

"Burn them?"

"As the soldiers did my mother," Thomas said sadly. "I will tend them."

"And me?" Elias asked, regaining his feet.

"Gather wood. We will light the lodge."

"It's far enough from the brush not to spread to the trees," Elias said, nodding. "But shouldn't we go back and tell Captain Rogers first? Shouldn't we—"

"They were my people," Thomas said, staring fiercely at Elias. "I will tend them."

Elias nodded sadly, then walked about, gathering broken branches and dry grass. As he stacked kindling near the door, he glanced inside. Thomas wrapped each of the stiff bodies in blankets or hides. He placed them together in the center of the room, then collected their belongings at their feet. Finally, as Elias announced the fire ready for lighting, Thomas chanted again.

"What does it mean?" Elias asked as Thomas struck the edge of his steel knife against a piece of dark flint. Sparks flew out, and after a few seconds, a bit of dry grass sprouted a flame. Soon dancing tongues of fire and smoke licked at the walls of the cabin, consuming the place in a brilliant ball of yellow and orange.

"It's hard to make over into your language," Thomas said as they retreated from the intensity of the blaze. "It . . . it has to be felt . . . felt here," Thomas said, putting his hand over Elias's heart. "It speaks of the short time a man walks the land. It tells of the gladness and the pain."

Elias nodded, and Thomas continued. But the words had little real meaning. Elias stared at the flames devouring the Riversnakes' cabin and remembered the hopes and dreams of little Andy and the others who'd come to the Brazos to learn farming and reading and writing. Were those dreams, like the cabin, to be swallowed by the cold of winter, devoured by the terrible jaws of hunger?

Elias remembered little of the slow ride homeward. Sometimes he would glance back at where the last of the embers had blazed. He and Thomas had shoved most of the glowing coals into the creek which lapped at the back edge of the cabin, fearing a sudden Brazos wind might send the flames into the trees. It had kept them there well into the deep of night, and Elias relied on the mule to know its way back to the barn.

"Elias?" his mother called when they at last approached the house. "Good Lord, Lias, what's kept you? Your father and the captain have been out looking for you boys!"

"We were at the Riversnakes' cabin," Elias explained.

"Captain Rogers said they saw smoke out that way," Mrs. Walsh said nervously. "He was afraid of Comanches—"

"We burned it," Elias said, trembling as he slid down from the saddle.

"Burned it?" his mother asked.

"They're all dead," Elias said, blinking the first tear from his eye. "Frozen. Starved."

"Won't be the last, I expect," spoke Captain Rogers, appearing suddenly in the middle of the road.

"No," Thomas agreed.

"We feared you boys lost," Elias's father said, dismounting from a tall roan cavalry mount. "The captain feared Comanches might have moved in on us. But then we saw the tracks—shod pony and two mules."

"I'm sorry if we worried you," Elias said, collapsing against his father.

"You've had a long day," Captain Rogers said, waving for the three soldiers behind him to dismount. "We'll talk tomorrow. For now, I'll see the stock tended. You boys get something to eat and find your beds."

"Yes, sir," Elias said.

Thomas nodded, and together they stumbled into the house, where Mrs. Walsh had a pot of stew bubbling.

Elias watched the others spoon stew into their mouths, but he himself ate little. His stomach seemed numb, his heart too swollen with sadness to leave room in his belly for food. He kept remembering Andy's gaunt cheeks, imagining the awful hunger that had crept upon the Riversnakes. Finally, Elias allowed his mother to take away the bowl.

"You'll feel better tomorrow," she said, gently stroking Elias's hair. But he doubted it. Nightmares had a way of lingering with him, especially when they became real.

Half the night he drifted in and out of an uneasy slumber. Sometimes he'd see Thomas tossing and turning a few feet away. Other times he'd imagine he saw a ghostly shadow walking outside, stretching out thin hands and moaning, "Come away with me. I'll take you to a place far away where you'll never be hungry again." The face then appeared, laughing with its dark eyes and snarling teeth. Soon it was a wolf, tearing at Elias's shoulder, ripping arms from their sockets, and . . .

He awoke, shivering and staring at the darkness. The air was crisp, cold in a way he'd never known before. For an instant he thought he was back in Galveston at his aunt's hotel, high up in the tower, alone, with no one to hear his eight-year-old sobs.

I'm not eight now, Elias told himself as he swallowed the would-be tears. There was a time when he could have rushed to his parents, begged them to cast away the sorrow or the fear. But Elias's father, like Thomas's Tonkawas, believed a man should be strong, even if he was only thirteen.

Elias plunged his head into the straw mattress and tried to cast away the demons of the night. Just then he would have welcomed the howls of a dozen wolves. Then, gazing out toward the door, he saw a white apparition step inside the barn. Slowly, undeniably, it made its way through the darkness until it knelt beside Elias's feet.

He wanted to shrink away, but he felt the sharp edge of the wolf's tooth against his chest. Courage, Thomas had said, flowed from that tooth. Elias lifted his head and stared into the eyes of his father.

It had been a long time since Peter Walsh had visited his son at night. Never so near dawn.

"What's this?" Elias's father asked, pulling at the buckskin line around Elias's neck until the wolf's tooth appeared.

"The wolf's tooth," Elias explained. "You remember. Thomas made it for me. It's like a rabbit's foot—good luck."

"You've had a hard day."

"Yes, sir," Elias whispered.

"Not sleeping too well tonight."

"No," Elias said, squeezing his father's hand. "It was seeing little Andy, I suppose, seeing him all covered with ice, frozen, thin as a fence rail. It was awful."

"Captain Rogers was right when he said there'll be more of that. You can't eat empty promises."

"Papa, can't you write somebody? What about the missions? Won't they send us help?"

"Mail doesn't get through, they tell me, Lias. Roads are

washed out. We'll find a way, though," the man said, running a warm hand along his son's side. "I've been praying."

"Papa, are you sure God's out there?"

"Son?"

"It seems to me there are so many terrible things happening. Thomas's mother and brothers died. The River-snakes. All the Caddos going hungry. Doesn't He care?"

"He sent you."

"Me?" Elias gasped. "Me?"

"You hunted the wolves. You brought meat. Who protected you from the wolves?"

"I don't understand."

"I'm not sure we ever do," Elias's father told him. "Any of us. I'm not certain why I left a comfortable home, a good job in Waco to come out here where the state government clearly doesn't want me, where the supplies never arrive, where my students aren't particularly eager to learn what I teach."

"You have doubts, Papa?"

"Often, especially when I see you in pain, Elias, and I don't know what to do."

"I'm all right."

"I know," Mr. Walsh said, gripping Elias's hand firmly. "But sometimes it's so hard to watch you growing tall, making mistakes, getting hurt—knowing I can't do anything to prevent it. I wish I could help you more, but . . ."

"I have to find my own path," Elias said, sitting up so that he could face his father eye to eye. "Thomas said that.

I'm not always sure about what he says, but he's right about that."

"Yes," Elias's father agreed.

"Papa, I used to hear you walking about at night back in Waco. Sometimes you'd look in through the door when you thought I wouldn't notice. What brought you in to-night?"

"I'm not certain, son," Mr. Walsh said, scratching his ear. "I saw you thrashing about, and I . . . well . . . just thought maybe you needed somebody around for a time."

Elias smiled, then lay back in bed as his father rose.

You were right, Papa, Elias thought as his father left. And glancing back at Thomas, even now tossing to and fro, Elias realized again the terrible burden loneliness placed on a person.

10.

Christmas came and went, but there was none of the usual good cheer. Few presents were exchanged, and dinner consisted of a rabbit stew Elias's mother and Alice Rogers concocted. It was a bleak time indeed, Elias thought.

The bitterest winds of winter passed, though, and as the sun rose brighter in the sky, wagons with provisions finally arrived from Fort Belknap. Even so, there was scarcely a surplus of anything. Wheat flour and cornmeal were portioned out, a keg of molasses was given each family, and a dozen milk cows were spread out among the Indian families so that milk and butter became available again. Later pigs and chickens followed.

Elias noticed more and more children returned to his father's schoolhouse. Even a few of the oldest boys appeared, though Thomas warned they would vanish again when the planting moon arrived. The younger boys did best, though, and Elias couldn't help swelling with pride when Austin Crowheart recited a whole page from Alice Rogers' modern poetry reader.

"I'm not sure Austin understood a word of it," Elias later confessed to Alice, "But he spoke the words terribly well."

"Yes," Alice agreed. "I wish the farming would come along as fast. Now, when the men should be clearing land for new fields, they run through the junipers seeking deer."

"It's hard for them," Elias told her. "Thomas says their people were good farmers once, but they've forgotten how. They miss the open plains."

"If they're not going to starve again next winter, they'd best apply themselves to clearing land," Alice declared, angrily stomping her foot. "There are people in Austin and Washington just hoping they'll fail. Don't they know that?"

"What people?" Elias asked nervously. "Who?"

"Nobody," Alice said, looking away. "I oughtn't talk."

She never did explain, but when Elias spoke to his father about it, Peter Walsh only laughed.

"The settlers to the east of us would as soon all the Indians were up north of the Red River," Elias's father told him. "There are people in the military that feel the same. But the worst of them have admitted we're making progress here, son. I wouldn't worry about it."

Actually Elias had little opportunity to concern himself with Alice's words. The next morning little Robert White-tail raced into the schoolhouse and shouted three harried Caddo words. Pure terror filled the boy from head to toe, and only Thomas was able to slow Robert's speech down to a speed that could be understood.

"Comanches?" Thomas asked, looking slightly skeptical.

Robert nodded and went on to say more. The other children soon began shrieking and running around the room, gathering their belongings and racing out the door.

"What's wrong?" Mr. Walsh cried out. "Boys, girls, stop!"

But whatever Robert was saying sent ripples of fear through the schoolhouse.

"He says he had a dream," Thomas finally told Elias after Robert had repeated his alarm. "He says a band of Comanches rode down along the river, scalping and burning, killing everyone in sight. He himself was running from one of them, and he could feel that Comanche's war club swing past his ear."

Robert knotted his fist and made a swishing sound. Then the boy crawled under one of the benches and lay perfectly still.

"Caddos take their dreams to be warnings," Thomas explained to a confused Mr. Walsh and a laughing Elias. "Robert says he saw Comanches here. We should make ready."

"You believe it's going to happen?" Elias asked.

"He does," Thomas explained, pointing to a cringing Robert Whitetail. "I've seen it this way. Someone has a dream. Later it happens just as they said."

"I'll see if I can locate Captain Rogers," Mr. Walsh said, reluctantly abandoning hope of continuing the lessons.

"Elias, you walk out to the barn and take that shotgun. Just in case."

"Yes, Papa," Elias said, leaving Thomas to cope with little Robert.

Captain Rogers sent a man to the fort to fetch soldiers. Meanwhile, Elias and Thomas agreed to set off to the south as scouts. The captain and Mr. Walsh headed north.

"All on account of a dream," Elias grumbled as they walked.

"Maybe we'll find a deer," Thomas said, slapping Elias on the back.

"I guess it's no worse than helping you with your numbers," Elias remarked.

"Perhaps Robert should dream more often."

They laughed together at the notion, then continued onward. Soon the noise of someone splashing through the water attracted their attention.

"Comanches?" Elias whispered.

Thomas said nothing, just motioned to load the shotgun and continue slowly. Elias's mind filled with a hundred images, each more frightening than the other. But as they threaded their way through the junipers, Elias saw no hint of horsemen. Instead they found themselves on a small hill overlooking a bend of the river. Below them were a half dozen Caddo maidens, all totally preoccupied with taking their weekly bath.

"They're . . ." Elias gasped.

"Yes," Thomas said, smiling. "Naked as they came into the world of light."

"I guess nobody'd mind if we watched awhile," Elias

said, sprawling out in the leaves. "After all, I don't see any danger."

"Maybe not from Comanches," Thomas whispered, "but you don't know their fathers."

Elias would have laughed except he was afraid of attracting attention. So instead of scouting out some Comanche war party, he and Thomas guarded the bathing maidens.

"The only trouble about this is we can't tell anyone," Elias complained as they headed home around noon. "If Mama discovered I'd . . ."

"Yes," Thomas said, grinning.

No Comanches were ever sighted in spite of Captain Rogers' sending out half a company on patrol. Ten five-man patrols turned up nary as much as a feather with Comanche markings, and life at the agency settled down.

In mid-March Elias celebrated his fourteenth birthday. Mrs. Walsh wrangled some extra sugar and baked a cake. Alice found some candles to decorate the cabin, and even Thomas joined in by cutting reed whistles so the boys at school could entertain Elias at midday.

There'd been better birthday celebrations, especially when Elias's brother and sisters were living at home, but certainly no event featured more surprises. Among the presents were a pair of new shirts Elias's mother had sewn, a small carving of a wolf from Thomas, a monogrammed handkerchief from Alice, and best of all, a spotted mustang pony from Elias's father and Captain Rogers.

"A wolf killer shouldn't spend his whole life riding a draft mule," the captain said, smiling broadly as he helped Elias into the saddle. "Now this brings me to the real question. While we were out patrolling for Comanches, we spotted a small herd of buffalo upriver. I thought to go after them, but I'd have to take a good scout, and young Thomas says he couldn't go unless you did. Well, Elias?"

"He's much too young," Mrs. Walsh objected.

"I'm fourteen, Mama," Elias said, sitting as tall and straight in the saddle as was possible.

"Peter, no," she said, gazing intently at her husband.

"Abbie, he's hunted wolves," Elias's father said. "Boys on the frontier have to hunt. A Caddo boy of fourteen would have ridden to the buffalo hunt. Besides, you know we need meat."

Mrs. Walsh sighed and shook her head, surrendering.

"It seems like the wind blows through and takes away their boyhood," she grumbled. "Just robs it like a thief."

As Elias prepared to set forth on the buffalo hunt, he didn't feel robbed of anything. It was as though he'd been presented with a special gift. He'd have the opportunity to ride the spotted horse he'd named Bucket, mainly because it delighted in knocking over the water buckets Elias and Thomas brought from the river.

"We will truly be warriors now," Thomas declared as he stripped off his agency clothes in favor of the long-neglected Tonkawa buckskins. "We'll be the first to find the buffalo, my friend. We'll be scouts, like my father."

Elias wasn't as excited by the prospect of riding ahead of the others and was pleased to discover Captain Rogers had assigned that duty to a redheaded private named Josefson.

"Has the sharpest eyes in the army," the captain boasted.

Thomas couldn't mask his disappointment.

"Private Josefson has already seen the herd," Elias explained.

"We are the youngest," Thomas reminded him. "The honor of scouting the herd should have been ours."

And no matter what Elias said, Thomas remained unreconciled to the fate of following along with the others. The only time Thomas betrayed even the hint of a smile was when Captain Rogers handed Elias and him each a shiny army rifle.

"Shotguns don't have a lot of effect on a buffalo," the captain explained. "You need the range between you and the horns. We'll practice some before we get too far. That way the recoil won't unhorse you."

Actually it did, twice. But it was better to find yourself sprawled out on the prairie when several thousand pounds of buffalo wasn't thundering down on you. The more they fired, the closer to the target Elias's ball would strike. The horses grew less skittish, too.

As they continued onward, Elias grew more confident. Around the campfire Thomas and the soldiers would swap dreadful stories of what terrifying fates had met this hunter or that. Soon the stories were swapped without a fire.

"Comanches," Thomas said, pointing to shadows moving across the twilight horizon.

When the herd was finally located, great care was taken to ensure the Comanches weren't around as well. Then, toward dusk, Thomas called them all together.

"My people believe the buffalo spirit gives of himself to feed and clothe us," Thomas said. "Always when we hunt, we say a prayer."

Thomas then raised his hands over his head and chanted. Once, twice, three times he cried out. Then he danced in a small circle, occasionally crying out to the stars. When he finished, he called his companions to gather in a circle.

"Hear me, buffalo spirit," Thomas said. "Make our bow arms strong. Give us the true aim. Give us your sons and daughters, that our children may grow strong. Shield us from the weakness that brings death."

Elias nodded, then said his own silent prayer that all would be well. Finally they all nestled into their blankets and waited for the challenge of the following morning.

When Elias awoke, he found the others busily saddling their horses or chewing a cold biscuit and some jerked beef. Elias joined in, grabbing some of the dried beef from his provision bag and hurrying to saddle Bucket lest he be left behind.

"Don't leave your rifle," Thomas said as Elias spread out the saddle blanket across the pony's back. "Stay close, my friend, for even a wolf's tooth can't shield you from a buffalo's horns."

Elias nodded, trying to fight the worry from his face. Dreadful stories surfaced in his mind, and he saw himself trampled or gored or dragged off by little Bucket. But in the end, Captain Rogers's clear, confident voice chased the worst of the fear away, and the wolf's tooth dangling around his neck disposed of the rest.

"There they are," Thomas whispered as the little band of horsemen topped a low ridge. "Don't fire until we are very close. Then shoot, turn, and ride away. Sometimes the bulls will turn on you. Then you ride fast into the trees. Buffalo don't like rocks and trees much. Their feet are made for the plains."

Elias digested the words and nodded to his friend. Moments later Captain Rogers waved his arm, and they set off down the slope toward the great woolies.

"E-yah!" Elias yelled as he followed Thomas toward a large black bull with huge horns. "E-yah!"

To Elias's dismay, the big bull seemed undisturbed. The other animals were making a slow turn, but the black bull stood motionless, grazing away as if he had not a care in the world. Then the first shot rang out, and a cow to the left of Captain Rogers fell.

"Now!" Thomas shouted, and he and Elias fired their rifles together. The motionless bull bawled out in pain, then stumbled forward. The rest of the buffalo continued circling, and Captain Rogers waved the soldiers toward that direction. Elias and Thomas were left to cope with the maddened black bull.

"I swore I hit him!" Elias yelled, hopelessly fumbling with the ramrod for his rifle.

"Yes," Thomas said, pointing at the large splotch of red on the bull's right shoulder. "Not a killing blow, but mine was lower. He will die, but not quickly."

"Like as not, he'll take us with him," Elias said as he turned Bucket away from the creature.

"No, stay with me," Thomas pleaded, stuffing the rifle into its saddle scabbard and pulling out a hunting knife.

"You'll get yourself killed," Elias declared. "You can't fight a bull buffalo with a hunting knife."

"It's not for that," Thomas said, climbing down and slashing a long branch from a young ash. "I'm making a spear."

They really had little time for chattering. The bull lumbered toward them, blood already streaming from his mouth and dripping into his beard.

"What do I do?" Elias asked.

"Reload, if you can," Thomas instructed. But even as the wounded beast plodded on, Elias saw the first traces of exhaustion appear. Suddenly, as if swept from his feet by the wind itself, the bull fell to one leg, then collapsed into a writhing dance of death.

"Are you reloaded?" Thomas asked. "Are you?"

"Just about," Elias said as he feverishly tried to make his fingers work faster than they were capable of working.

"Shoot! Shoot, Elias!"

Elias rammed home the padding, then aimed and fired. The buffalo turned to stare at its tormentor, then dropped lifelessly to the ground.

By the time the hunt had ended, seven of the hairy creatures were dead. Their hides were cut away, and the meat was dressed and packed aboard spare animals. Soon the little hunting party appeared among the Indians, meting out buffalo shoulders or haunches to families, smaller pieces to individuals.

A quarter was saved for Elias's mother, and an equal portion went to Captain Rogers. The soldiers carried meat back to the fort as well.

As Elias watched his mother cut strips for five steaks, he laughed.

"Alice is making dinner for her father, Mama," he told her. "There are just four of us—me, you, Papa, and Thomas."

"We have a surprise guest, Elias," she said, shaking her head. "Major Neighbors is here."

"He is?" Elias asked, scratching his head. "I thought he only came down when something important needed deciding. What's wrong?"

"Nothing that I know of," Mrs. Walsh said. "He likes to visit the school."

"But he never stays to dinner. He wants to speak to Captain Rogers. Is—"

"That's enough, Elias," she said, laughing at him. "He's allowed to stay when he feels the urge. Now clean yourself up and prepare for dinner. Understand?"

"Yes, ma'am," Elias said, scowling as he left.

11.

Major Neighbors stayed but two days, then left with a small cavalry patrol. Neither the major nor Captain Rogers hinted that anything had changed, but even Elias could tell they were worried. But with meat to distribute and hides to treat, not to mention his regular duties at the school, Elias had little time to devote to anything else.

As spring raced toward summer, the number of students at the school dwindled steadily. First there was the planting. Later came the thinning of plants, the tending of gardens. Some days no more than a handful of children worked at their lessons. Once Elias and Thomas had the entire schoolhouse to themselves.

Seeing the schoolhouse near empty did little to impress the visitors who once again flocked to the agency. A steady trickle of settlers passed through as well. Often Elias would listen as they eyed the cornstalks growing taller in the nearby fields.

"If you ask me," one of them said, "this good land is wasted on a bunch of Indians. All they really want to do is scalp our womenfolk. We'd be well rid of them altogether."

"Let 'em enjoy it while they can," another declared. "They won't be here for long. They're all headed for the Nations. Let 'em stay up there with the Cherokees!"

Thomas never said a word about those comments, but Elias could tell they stung.

"That wouldn't be fair," Elias told his friend. Thomas merely nodded and continued to work.

Major Neighbors returned in May with a delegation from Austin, the state capital. Two soldiers had come ahead to warn Captain Rogers, and Thomas had made a special trip to Indian Springs to ensure good attendance at school.

Elias's father smiled broadly as Austin Crowheart and the Jackson boys recited their alphabet and read passages from the McGuffey readers. The wife of a state senator clapped wildly, and the senator himself made a speech after Thomas solved a math problem.

"I knew these young Indians could learn if given the chance," the senator said, smiling at anyone and everyone. "It's as I told the governor. Put them on the path to civilization, and they'll make good citizens."

Most of the visitors were less enthusiastic. They spoke of Comanche raiding parties, of men, women, and children brutally attacked.

"All this is well and good," the governor's representative told Mr. Walsh. "But educating a dozen Caddos solves nothing. If you had a hundred Comanches in there, we'd still feel safer with the tribes moved on north of the Red River."

Major Neighbors and Captain Rogers spent long hours arguing with several delegates. When the major led the party of visitors back to Fort Belknap, both he and the captain appeared dour-faced.

"They're worried," Alice told Elias the next morning. "I can tell. Really worried. But I'm afraid to know what it's about."

Elias often caught his parents whispering quietly. As soon as he approached, they would grow silent. The whispering continued for a week, growing worse each time a group of visitors appeared at the schoolhouse.

"Papa, what's happening?" Elias asked after dinner one night. "Is everything all right?"

"Everything's just fine," Elias's mother said, speaking more to Thomas than to her son. "We've had problems before. We'll find a solution."

"Problems?" Elias asked. "What problems? Everyone's well fed. The supplies have been on time since March. The crops are doing fine."

"Nothing you should worry over," Mrs. Walsh said, squeezing Elias's neck. "Nor you, Thomas."

The second week of June Major Neighbors arrived with a captain from the quartermaster's corps. They didn't visit the school. Instead they rode through the Indian camps, making notes of all kinds. When they finally left, Elias found his mother alone in the cabin, her eyes red and swollen from crying.

"Mama?" he asked. "What's happened?"

"They're closing the agencies, both here and on the Clear Fork," she told him.

"Closing them?" Elias gasped.

"All the tribes are to be sent across the Red River."

"And if they won't go?"

"They'll have to go," Mrs. Walsh said, clasping Elias's hand firmly. "The Second Cavalry will escort them."

"When?" Elias asked. "After harvest?"

"Soon," she said. "Before the crops come in. Your father thinks the settlers nearby are envious of the corn crop. They want to do the harvesting themselves. It's a fine way to do business, bring in the harvest that others have planted and tended."

"Maybe we should fight it," Elias suggested. "Most of the Caddos have rifles."

"No," she said sadly. "The tribal elders have already agreed. Not that there was any real choice. It's move or die. We put so much effort into making the agency a success. Now it's all for nothing. Your papa is heartbroken."

"What about us, Mama? Are we going to stay?"

"No, Lias. We'll go north to Fort Belknap for the balance of your papa's contract. Then I suspect we'll return to Waco, or head to St. Louis maybe."

"Does Thomas know?" Elias asked quietly.

"Captain Rogers told him. They've gone to inform the others."

"It's going to be hard for him to understand," Elias said, thinking at the same time that it was hard for anyone to understand something like this, something that made no sense.

"He's your friend," Mrs. Walsh reminded Elias. "Help

him if you can. It's not always easy for Thomas to share his pain. Maybe with you he'll . . ."

"I know," Elias said, turning toward the door. "I'll talk to him." Then Elias headed outside to find Thomas Three Feathers.

Tracking down an Indian, especially one who didn't particularly want to be found, was never an easy task. Elias saddled his pony and rode through half the camps along the river. He finally located Thomas beside the charred remains of the Riversnakes' cabin.

"I've been looking for you," Elias said, rolling off the side of the horse.

"I was with Captain Rogers," Thomas explained. "He had words for the others."

"And for you?" Elias asked.

Thomas nodded, and the two boys walked silently together along the creek bank for a few minutes. Finally Thomas stopped, and Elias placed a shaky hand on the Tonkawa's broad shoulder.

"I don't know what to say," Elias whispered. "It doesn't seem fair."

"It's like all treaties," Thomas said, gazing out at the distant line of hills. "Words on paper. The only truth is found in a man's heart."

Elias felt a shudder wind its way through his friend, but Thomas remained stonefaced.

"What will you do?" Elias asked. "Go with your father?"

"I don't know," Thomas said, shaking loose of Elias's hand. "Who can tell?"

"Maybe you could stay with us? Mama says we're going

to Fort Belknap. Your father might even be sent there."

"It's no good to plan," Thomas said, turning toward Elias at last. "I know your heart, Elias. You want to share this pain, but it is mine to bear."

"We're friends."

"Yes," Thomas said, his lip quivering. "But our paths are different."

"You mean because I'm white?" Elias asked. "I can't help that. It didn't keep us from hunting the wolves together, from sharing the buffalo hunt. I helped you learn your figures, and you taught me how to make snares and work hides. I don't feel we're different, Thomas. It's like we're brothers."

"Yes," Thomas said somberly. "I know. We are one heart, you and me. But that may change."

"No!" Elias shouted. "I know you think I'll forget, but I won't. I haven't seen my brother Joshua in more than a year, but I still remember the things we did together. Besides, I've got reminders."

Elias opened his shirt and pointed to the thin red lines across his chest made by the wolf's claws. Thomas touched the scars, then opened his own shirt. Elias frowned. Yes, there were scars there, too, marks Elias had seen often. But in all the time they'd known each other, Thomas had never shared their origin. He did now.

"I was very small," Thomas began. "Too small maybe for my father to have taken me to hunt the deer, but I was his son, and he wished to show me his skill as a hunter. He shot two deer, and we made camp. In the night they came."

"White men?" Elias asked.

"Yes," Thomas said, nodding sadly. "My father fought them, but they were three, and he only one. They took the deer, and when I rose to stop them, one cut me with a knife. As long as I live, I will bear the mark of that night. Its memory is with me always."

Elias frowned, then gazed at the stars overhead.

"The white man has brought me pain and sorrow, Elias," Thomas continued, "and you can't change that. It's not your doing."

"I want to help, though."

"Yes, I know," Thomas said, shaking off the hurt and managing to grin. "Come," he added, leading the way to two small boulders. He sat down on one, and Elias seated himself on the other.

"When I was very small," Thomas said, "my father took me to a place far from our camp. He built a fire. As it burned, he told me of our people, of the Tonkawas who once rode the land, tall and proud. He then marked my hand."

Thomas revealed three small scars on his wrist, each taking the appearance of a feather.

"Three feathers," Elias whispered. "Your name."

"So that I would always know who I am," Thomas explained.

"How was it done?" Elias asked. "With a knife?"

"Burned," Thomas said softly. "With a stick."

"Then I guess we'd better build a fire," Elias said soberly. "Will it hurt much?"

"I don't remember. Maybe. Your mother will not like it."

"She'll understand."

Thomas didn't appear convinced, but Elias began gathering dry leaves and branches for the fire. Thomas took out his knife and struck it against his flint. As the fire consumed the smallest of the twigs, Elias prepared for the pain.

"You're not afraid?" Thomas asked as Elias turned his head away from the fire.

"A little," Elias admitted. "It couldn't be as bad as that wolf slicing me open, though."

Thomas smiled for the first time that afternoon, and Elias grinned back. Later, when Thomas pressed the blazing end of a branch against the pale, tender flesh of Elias's wrist, the grin faded. Instinctively Elias pulled his hand away from the sudden pain, and Thomas almost dropped the red-hot branch in Elias's lap. Finally Elias placed his hand against a rock, and Thomas tried a second time. The pain was fierce, but it was quickly over. The second and third feathery scars were somewhat easier. When the mark was complete, Elias raced to the creek and plunged his hand into the cooling waters.

"Aaaaah!" Elias screamed, letting the pain flow from his hand. Thomas broke open some brownish berries and spread a soothing liquid across the inflamed wrist.

"Now we are brothers," Thomas said, gripping Elias's shoulders firmly and chanting to the sky. "Will you stay with me tonight?"

"Here?" Elias asked. "Mama and Papa will fret. We'll both catch it tomorrow."

"I must," Thomas explained, slapping his chest. "But you can return. Tell your father I will come back when the sun rises."

"I'll stay," Elias said, reading the intensity in his friend's eyes.

"Good," Thomas said, smiling again.

They didn't speak much the rest of the afternoon, just stared at the far hills or listened to the songs of the cardinals and the chattering squirrels in the trees overhead. It grew dark, and hunger gnawed at Elias's empty belly. But Thomas said nothing, just walked along the creek and gazed skyward. Finally, as the moon rose over a darkened land, Thomas walked to the edge of the creek and stripped off his clothes.

"Isn't it late for a swim?" Elias asked.

"It's how I pray, Elias," Thomas explained. "I speak to the spirits in the sky, asking that they help me find my way."

Elias sat quietly and watched as Thomas stood naked in the moonlight, screaming Tonkawa words at the clouds. The wind stirred Thomas's long black hair, and the waters of the creek seemed to surge back and forth in answer.

"This is my brother, Elias, who wears the wolf's tooth," Thomas then spoke. "Walk with us both, spirits, for ours is a difficult path."

A large cloud seemed to swallow the moon, and the faint light disappeared. Soon the moon reappeared, and Elias felt a strange tingling sensation.

"It's well," Thomas said, turning away from the water. "We can return."

Elias nodded, though he understood almost none of it. All he could think of was the charred flesh of his wrist and the terrible hunger that was growing in his belly.

12.

Word of the great movement north across the Red River spread like wildfire along the Texas frontier. It seemed to Elias that each day some settler happened by for a final look at the agency. Or perhaps Captain Rogers was closer to the truth.

"They're having a look at the farms, seeing if they might like to take a hand in the bidding."

Elias walked around with a heavy heart. Few children attended his father's classes. Most were occupied with the tasks of readying themselves for yet another long journey from a land that had for the shortest of times been home. As summer baked the land, Elias was surprised to see many of the Indians still tending their fields. Maybe they think it won't happen after all, he told himself. Or maybe it wasn't in their hearts to watch the cornstalks wither and die along with their once high hopes.

Thomas continued his lessons as though nothing had happened. If anything, the young Tonkawa progressed more than before. Thomas had a true talent for reading, and as his hand became more familiar with a quill, his writing grew to be clear and precise. Figures continued to trouble him, but Elias was certain that with practice Thomas would be the equal of anyone in the state.

It was in the quiet hours of the evening that Elias noticed his friend most changed. Often Thomas would disappear for hours. More than once Elias happened upon Thomas standing beside the river, reaching with his arms toward the heavens and uttering some somber, tearful cry.

"He's afraid," Elias told his father. "Can't he stay with us, Papa? He'd work for his keep."

"I'd like to ask him, Elias, but you told me yourself," Mr. Walsh reminded his son. "He has his path, and we have ours."

Finally Captain Rogers announced grimly that the great exodus would begin in three days, and cavalrymen arrived with wagons to carry belongings.

"I'm to go," Thomas told Elias. "I will interpret for my people."

"Most of them speak pretty fair English now," Elias pointed out. "Austin Crowheart and the Jackson boys almost as good as you."

"Long ago, my friend, I learned not to question what the spirits decide. I go where I am blown, as a leaf in the autumn."

It was a sad image, Thomas cast to the whims of fate. Elias tried not to think of his friend all alone in that strange land to the north, walking beside some stream, perhaps hearing the cries of the wolves, knowing there was no companion to share the dangers.

The night before Thomas was to leave, Elias slept little. In the morning, after bundling Thomas's meager possessions in a blanket, the two boys made their way to the river as always. But instead of filling their buckets and returning to the barn, they shed their clothes and waded into the cool waters of the Brazos.

"You swim better," Thomas said as they splashed into deeper water.

"You write and read," Elias replied.

"We've taught each other," Thomas said, grinning. "That's how it should be with brothers."

Elias glanced at the three small scars on his wrist, at the larger marks on his chest, then nodded.

Later, as they lay in the soft meadow grass of the riverbank, Thomas frowned. It seemed the Indian was older, suddenly aged by a terrible sadness. When Thomas touched the scars, Elias forced a smile onto his face.

"They'll help me remember," Elias said.

"Don't remember what you see there," Thomas said, shaking his head. "Remember what you feel . . . here," he added, pounding his chest. "That is where we will always be brothers."

"I don't understand why they're sending you away from here," Elias finally cried out in frustration. "I can't see why you can't stay."

"We do as the soldiers decide."

"They shouldn't be the ones deciding!" Elias shouted.

"Someone always decides," Thomas said, grabbing Elias's hand. "When you are small, your father or mother says what will be. You don't question. You do as you're told."

"It's hard sometimes, though," Elias said, rubbing a tear from his eye. "Especially when you know it's wrong."

"I grow angry about it, too. But then I think of my friend, Elias, who worries, and I know mine is not the only difficult path. My people, the Tonkawa, fade like the evening sun. We won't rise again with dawn, I fear. We, like the sun, can be swallowed by the clouds. But another sun will follow, my friend."

"Maybe one day you'll ride down to Fort Belknap and visit me. Or I'll ride north to the reservation."

"Maybe," Thomas said, gazing off across the river at the cliffs towering over the opposite bank. "But if not, don't worry. I'll be off chasing the buffalo or hunting with the wolf."

"Yes, the wolf," Elias said, fingering the single tooth dangling from his neck. "Here." Elias removed the necklace and passed it to his friend. "It's you who's going to need the heart of the wolf now. It's going to take lots of courage to go north."

Thomas placed the charm around his neck and smiled somberly. The two boys gripped hands, and for an instant, it was as if they were one. Elias thought he heard something across the river, a cry not unlike that of a wolf. Suddenly, that night they'd sat together in the barn and listened to it seemed a lifetime in the past.

"I won't forget," Elias promised as Thomas finally pulled away.

"I know," Thomas said sadly.

That same afternoon Elias stood with his father and watched the sad column of disinherited Indians pass by the river. There were Tonkawas, Anadarkos, and especially Caddos, the stiff-lipped people who had given the state its name. *Tejas,* the Spaniards had written it. "Friend." Elias read traces of that elusive friendship in the faces of the little ones, in the reluctant farewell waves of Sam Jackson and little Robert Whitetail. Austin Crowheart rode by on a pony, naked except for trousers cut off at the knees. Elias doubted if civilization would have any permanent effect.

"We'll be going ourselves tomorrow," Elias's father said. "I suppose you would have enjoyed riding part of the way with Thomas, but I don't want to feel like we are a part of this. I want to believe that some fragment of what we've built here will go on."

"It doesn't matter, Papa," Elias said. "With or without us, they're going. And after we're gone, someone will buy this land and harvest the crops, live in the cabins, swim in the river."

Elias walked a few feet away and touched his neck. He felt naked without the necklace. It had been there so long it'd become a part of him. Still, he knew Thomas needed it more.

Elias found himself searching the long line of plodding wagons for his friend. Thomas finally appeared, riding alongside Major Neighbors. Yes, there was Thomas, bare-chested, the wolf's tooth plainly in view. Suddenly Thomas reared up his horse and charged through the line, screaming out at the startled soldiers guarding the flank, and heading straight for where Elias stood.

"Ayyyy!" Thomas cried out, pulling his pony to a halt. Elias, without thinking, jumped up behind Thomas, and together they rode off down the hillside. Thomas stopped his horse halfway between the hill and the wagons.

"Yes," Elias said, climbing down. "I have to stay."

"And I have to go," Thomas said, reaching his hand down so that it met Elias's grasping fingers. "Raven, my mother's brother, once told me the world is a great circle. You take your path, little brother, and I take mine. But one day we will meet, for surely all paths must cross."

"Surely," Elias agreed, reluctantly releasing Thomas's hand.

The column moved on, and Thomas with it. Elias watched them vanish beyond the far horizon. Then he slowly turned and began the walk back toward his parents. It was time to bid farewell to that which had been. Once again the moment had arrived to begin anew.

About the Author

G. CLIFTON WISLER is the author of twenty-five books for adults and young people, many of them about the American West. A resident of Garland, Texas, he currently teaches English to eighth graders at Bowman Middle School in nearby Plano.

About this book, the author says: "My mind often takes me back to that earlier time when the struggle for daily survival required something extra from the men and women—and yes, the children too—of the Texas frontier. I'm always interested in little-known episodes of Texas history, and the story of the Belknap Indian Reservation is one that offered all sorts of opportunities for drama."